THE "FRENCH WRITE[RS OF] CANADA" SERIES

The purpose of this series is to bring to English readers, for the first time, in a uniform and inexpensive format, a selection of outstanding and representative works by French authors in Canada. Individual titles in the series will range from the most modern work to the classic. Our editors have examined the entire repertory of French fiction in this country to ensure that each book that is selected will reflect important literary and social trends, in addition to having evident aesthetic value.

Current Titles in the Series

Ethel and the Terrorist, a novel by Claude Jasmin, translated by David Walker.
The Temple on the River, a novel by Jacques Hébert, translated by Gerald Taaffe.
Ashini, a novel by Yves Thériault, translated by Gwendolyn Moore.
N'tsuk, a novel by Yves Thériault, translated by Gwendolyn Moore.
The Torrent, novellas and short stories by Anne Hébert, translated by Gwendolyn Moore.
Dr. Cotnoir, a novel by Jacques Ferron, translated by Pierre Cloutier.
Fanny, a novel by Louis Dantin, translated by Raymond Chamberlain.
The Saint Elias, a novel by Jacques Ferron, translated by Pierre Cloutier.

(Continued)

"THE FRENCH WRITERS OF CANADA" SERIES (continued)

The Juneberry Tree, a novel by Jacques Ferron, translated by Raymond Chamberlain.

Jos Carbone, a novel by Jacques Benoit, translated by Sheila Fischman.

The Grandfathers, a novel by Victor-Lévy Beaulieu, translated by Marc Plourde.

In an Iron Glove, volume one of the autobiography of Claire Martin, translated by Philip Stratford.

The Right Cheek, volume two of the autobiography of Claire Martin, translated by Philip Stratford.

The Forest, a novel by Georges Bugnet, translated by David Carpenter.

The Poetry of Modern Quebec: an Anthology, edited and translated by Fred Cogswell.

The Brawl, a novel by Gérard Bessette, translated by Marc Lebel and Ronald Sutherland.

Marie Calumet, a novel by Rodolphe Girard, translated by Irène Currie.

Master of the River, a novel by Félix-Antoine Savard, translated by Richard Howard.

Bitter Bread, a novel by Albert Laberge, translated by Conrad Dion.

The Making of Nicolas Montour, a novel by Léo-Paul Desrosiers, translated by Christina Roberts.

(and many more)

The Brawl

by
GÉRARD BESSETTE

translated by
Marc Lebel and
Ronald Sutherland

HARVEST HOUSE
Montreal

Advisory Editor.

Ben-Zion Shek,
Department of French,
University of Toronto.

Copyright© 1976 by Harvest House Ltd.
First Harvest House Edition —
October 1976.
Deposited in the Bibliothèque Nationale of
Québec, 4th quarter, 1976.
Originally published in the French language
by Le Cercle du Livre de France Ltée, Montreal
in 1958, as *La Bagarre*.
The present translation is based
on the 1969 CLF edition.

For information, address Harvest House Ltd.
4795 St. Catherine St. W., Montreal,
Quebec H3Z 2B9

Series design by Robert Reid.
Cover illustration: Linda Kooluris

The Publishers gratefully acknowledge a
translation grant from The Canada Council.

Canadian Cataloguing in Publication Data
      Bessette, Gérard, 1920 —
         [La Bagarre. English]
         The Brawl
         (The French writers of Canada series)
         Translation of La Bagarre.
         ISBN paper 88772-1699 (cloth) 88772-227X
      I. Title. II. Title: La Bagarre. English. III. Series.
      PS8503   C843'.5'4   C76-015010-9
      PQ3919.2.B49B313

THE BRAWL

Part One

I

"Say what you like, it's a pain in the arse," stated Lebeuf, his eyes riveted to his glass of whiskey as he slowly turned it between his huge hands.

Weston nodded and streched his legs lazily under the table. His piercing greenish eyes, separated by a short flat nose, gave him the appearance of an owl.

"Yeah," he replied in his native American English. Then in a rather singing tone, he continued in French, "I understand your predicament." He let his gaze wander around the interior of the Blue Sky Cafe, with its bluish stucco walls lit by Chinese-style lanterns shaped like crescents. "Touchy situation."

Lebeuf raised his head. The light from the lanterns left shadows on the wrinkled brow over his gray, expressionless eyes.

"A hundred percent pain in the arse," he repeated glumly in his thick Quebec accent. He drank down his whiskey and wiped his heavy lips with the back of his hand. "Hundred percent."

Weston took his pipe out of his pocket and packed it carefully. "Of course, you could... how do you say 'dump her'?"

Lebeuf shrugged his shoulders. "Easy enough to say..."

His gaze wandered for a moment through the smoke-filled room. All around him, drinkers seated at small, round tables without tablecloths sipped their beer and looked bored. Further back, on a platform, a skeleton-like Negro was playing a rhumba on the piano.

"…but not easy to do." Weston had lit his pipe and was puffing out smoke rings between his thin lips. "I know. I had a girl, too, in France, before I broke my leg. She wanted to come back to the States with me after the war." He broke into English again. "I dumped her."

The Negro's rhumba came to an end. He greeted the audience, waving his clenched hands over his head like a boxer, and then broke into the "Beer Barrel Polka." A few couples advanced toward the dance floor.

"Yeah," said Lebeuf, emptying his glass, "but it's not the same. You weren't living with her."

Weston nodded. A short, blond lock of hair fell over his forehead. "No."

"When you're shacked up it's another story," said Lebeuf. The idiom he used was *"c'est une autre paire de manches."*

The American pulled a notebook out of his pocket and made a note: *"c'est une autre paire de manches;* it's another story, a different situation."

He cast a satisfied glance at the other expressions gleaned throughout the day and said, "It's always hard to... how would you put it in French — 'shake off.' "

Lebeuf thought for a few seconds. " *'Faire lâcher,'* I suppose."

"Good, *'faire lâcher une femme.'* But they get over it. Take my word for it, Jules."

"Yeah." The big man hailed a passing waiter. "Two more the same."

Then he turned to the American. "When you're shacked up, it's not the same, Ken." Jules was getting fed up with Weston's rather skeptical pout. "Do you think

8

there's any way you can work in a room when there's a woman always standing next to you? Go ahead and try it! You come home one night. You've made up your mind to do something. You sit at a table, you grab a pen, you start thinking about what you want to say, then all of a sudden, dammit, the radio starts squawking, or it's the chick herself who starts blabbering. Can't write a bloody word. So you grab your hat and coat and bugger off. Nothin'else to do.'' Lebeuf suddenly stopped and started rolling his glass between his hairy hands again.

Weston gazed at his massive face for a few moments, the bulging eyes and the two vertical lines which joined each side of his nose to the edge of his mouth. ''I suppose you used to write before?''

Jules' face became somber. He tugged at the collar of his pullover. ''Wasn't ready then.'' He went back to contemplating his glass. His face expressed only weariness.

''It's hard to do three things at once,'' said Weston.

''Yeah. Excuses for not doing anything can always be found. But you, anyway, at least you write.''

Ken burst out laughing. ''If you can call a thesis writing.''

''But you do write,'' insisted the big man.

''I make notes; it's not the same.''

''Anyway, you're doing something; you know where you're going.''

''That's where you're wrong. I don't have a clue. That's why it's such a pain. A thesis on French Canadians. Do you have any idea of what that involves...''

They were interrupted by a shrill voice. ''Gentlemen, we are dreadfully sorry to interrupt your learned discourses and beg to be granted the honor of joining your fraternal bash.''

Lebeuf and Weston raised their heads. Augustin Sillery

stood before them, his arms spread out like a conductor holding a note, his chest puffed out under a rust-colored jacket, his collar held up with a bow tie. He had a young, baby-faced student with him.

"It goes without saying, gentlemen, that I cannot hope to make any contribution unless liquid or spirituous to your dignified dissertations." Sillery cast a glance toward the young student and went on in a falsetto voice. "However, since I know how to embrace the divine bottle as well as anyone here, I shall force myself, whilst guzzling assiduously, to lend an attentive ear to the words which flow from your eloquent lips."

"Sit down, will you," said Lebeuf rather annoyed. "You're gonna wear yourself out."

"Your solicitude, my dear, moves me to my very viscera..." He quickly stood aside to offer a seat to young Langevin, who looked rather unsteady, and ordered a round of whiskey. "I was just in the midst, sirs, of explaining to this young man the circumstances which led to my developing an Oedipus complex..."

Langevin broke into a drawn-out laugh, as Sillery, with nostrils quivering, threw out his chest. "It was during the horror of the dead of night," his tragic voice continued, "as my pater, no doubt moved by the blooming of the first daisies, tried..."

"Yeah," interrupted Lebeuf, "we've heard that one before."

Augustin bit his lip and gave the big fellow an indignant look.

"Let him go on," said Weston with a smile. "I'm getting myself an education here. Go on, Augustin."

Augustin's chest heaved in a long deep sigh. He had regained his composure. "Nothing would give me more pleasure, my dear sir, than to acquiesce in your request, but I understand full well that for a novelist of the caliber

10

of our distinguished colleague," he gestured limply toward Lebeuf, "my modest analyses are nothing but goat turds, a sort of, how should I..."

"Enough," said Lebeuf, "when I want your comments, I'll ask for them."

"But never would I dare, my dear sir! If ever you did deign to submit to my enraptured eyes but a few lines from your pen, I would prostrate myself forehead to the ground and admire in utter silence."

Weston cast a worried glance toward the big man. "Let's not waste our drinks," he said, lifting his glass.

Sillery grabbed his glass and clinked it with Langevin's. "Right you are, let us drain our glasses of this vile fluid. It is a source of inspiration and liberation with no equal."

"Let us drain our glasses," repeated the watery-eyed Langevin.

"Ah, but be careful, young man!" warned Sillery, holding back Langevin's arm. "Let us not consider these libations, however sacred, as an end in themselves. They constitute but one of the means available to us to liberate our inner selves. Let us practice in its fullness the Rimbaudian immoderation."

A drum roll interrupted him. The skeletal piano player was finishing his number. Four musicians came up on the stage. Dancers scurried onto the dance floor. The trombone emitted a long caterwaul, the cymbals and the drums resounded, supported by saxophone and clarinet.

"Gentlemen," shouted Sillery, "would it not be infinitely more fitting for us to transport our household gods beneath a more hospitable roof? The inauthenticity of this syncopated music is in no way propitious to the subtleties of psychoanalysis."

"La Bougrine is the only place," said Lebeuf.

"Then off to La Bougrine!"

11

Langevin got up first and with an unsteady step headed for the exit.

II

La Bougrine was different from the other Montreal night-clubs. Instead of an impersonal, American-style setting, the interior was set up as a lumber camp. The walls were made of logs. Huge, rough beams ran along the ceiling, and a few oil lamps were suspended from them. All around the hall hung trappers' boots, snowshoes, home-spun parkas and rawhide boots. The long, poorly planed wooden tables could accommodate twenty guests and had barrel-shaped seats on either side. The waiters wore tuques with pompoms, moccasins and loggers' clothes. The floorshow, which was entirely in French, featured square-dancing, country songs and double-entendre jokes.

Since La Bougrine had recently been highlighted in an American tourist guide, it hosted a rather impressive American clientele. The sudden influx of tourists had brought in its wake an array of self-appointed translators who, for tips and drinks, would translate the floorshow's songs and jokes for the benefit of their English-speaking clients.

It was two o'clock in the morning when the four companions walked into the "rustic" club. Sillery sat next to Langevin and, an arm wrapped round his shoulder, started to whisper something in his ear. Comfortably seated at the end of the table, facing Weston, Lebeuf was rubbing his hands with satisfaction.

"Yeah, it sure cheers you up!" he said, scanning the hall.

Ken thought differently. "This is only the third time I've been here, but I think it's just a tourist trap, just like our fake western bars and our gangster joints in Chicago."

A waiter came over to take their order.

"Whiskey, pardner," said Lebeuf. "Somethin' real stiff. We're not tourists, you know. The difference between the States and Quebec," he went on, turning to Weston, "is precisely that you've had a bellyful of cowboys and gangsters. I suppose it must get on your nerves when some stranger wants to make you talk about Hollywood or Chicago, while for us..."

"Right!"

"Okay, but all that stuff, at least it's something. It pisses you off maybe, but when the stereotypes of a country spread around like that just about everywhere, it's a good sign."

"A good sign! In Europe we're passed off for a bunch of savages!"

"It's better than being passed off for nothing. The Frenchmen don't even know we curse here in Canada."

Weston shrugged his shoulders. Apparently, he did not see the importance of such a peculiarity.

"Just a minute," sneered Lebeuf. "It's quite easy to say you don't give a damn when you belong to a great big country. But when foreigners start drawing cartoons it means they're interested in the original."

The husky fellow swilled down his whiskey and took another look round the hall. A few Anglophones were mouthing off at each other, making wild gestures. Other drinkers were nodding sleepily over their glasses, waiting for the next show. Next to Langevin, Sillery was scribbling something on a piece of paper. On the stage, two

14

fiddlers were scraping out a jig and tapping their feet.

Lebeuf emptied another full glass and turned to Weston. "An Italian," he said, "has a handlebar moustache and eats spaghetti singing an opera tune; a Frenchman shakes everybody's hand and lifts up petticoats; an Englishman, tight-assed in his dinner jacket, contemplates the Empire from behind his monocle; an American tosses off a few highballs while shooting off his revolver; a Canadian doesn't do anything."

Weston guffawed. "Not bad," he said in English.

With an air of modesty Lebeuf ran his hand through his brush-cut. He was proud of this tirade, which he had written down the evening before in his notebook. *If I only had time* he said to himself. *If only Marguerite wasn't there. I've got pretty good ideas sometimes.*

"But, no kidding," the American went on, "I just can't see why you're wracking your brains with that type of thing. All we do in the States is live. To hell with..."

A shrill song cut him off. The drinkers turned around. Standing on a chair not far from the giggling Langevin, Sillery was breaking into a tune with a rather pleasant tenor voice.

> *Un Canadien errant,*
> *Banni de ses foyers*
> *Parcourant en fourrant*
> *Des bordels étrangers!*

"Hurrah!"

"Shut up, Joe. He's singing a real native folksong. Very characteristic you know."

"I adore these little ditties!"

At every table, conversation had stopped. Hurriedly a few interpreters were trying to explain *"Un Canadien errant."*

"Patriotic song, you know..."

"Christ, get up on the table so we can hear it better."

Sillery did so and carried on.

> *Un jour, triste et pensif*
> *Couché sur une peau*
> *Au courant fugitif*
> *Il adressa ces mots.*

The dismayed interpreters were suddenly assailed with questions and made an effort to translate on the spot.

"He is in the bed, you know, wit'..."

One of them even had to struggle in Spanish for the benefit of a few Mexicans:

"*Es en cama con sa querida y...*"

"*Bravo! Muy interesante!*"

A few customers bawled out in chorus:

> *Au courant fugitif*
> *Il adressa ces mots...*

The student felt encouraged to go on.

> *Si tu deviens pipi,*
> *O déduit chaleureux,*
> *Je me ferai fifi*
> *On fait ce que l'on peut!**

"*Je me ferai fifi. On fait ce que l'on peut,*" roared the audience. There were thundering rounds of applause.

*Sillery's song is a take-off on a well-known and oft-parodied French-Canadian folksong. In the original it goes:

Un Canadien errant	A wandering Canadian
Banni de ses foyers	Banished from his ho.ne
Parcourait en pleurant	Went wandering and crying
Des pays étrangers.	Through foreign lands.

His arms stretched out pleading for silence, Sillery remained on his roost. "Ladies and gentlemen, if you'll be so kind as to accord me a few minutes of your gracious attention, I shall explain for the benefit of your distinguished American and Spanish guests a few obscure passages of the third verse..."

"He'll explain the third couplet," whispered an interpreter.

"It is of primordial importance to start by attempting the exegesis of certain terms which, without being so to speak esoterical, need nonetheless to be elucidated..."

"What the hell's he talkin' about?" said an American tourist who had thus far prided himself on understanding French.

Un jour, triste et pensif,	One day, sad and thoughtful,
Assis au bord des flots	Sitting by the seaside,
Au courant fugitif	To the fugitive current
Il adressa ces mots:	He addressed these words:
Si tu vois mon pays,	If you see my country,
Mon pays malheureux,	My unhappy country,
Va dire à mes amis	Go tell my friends
Que je me souviens d'eux.	That I remember them.
Oh, mais en expirant,	Oh, but when I'm dying,
Mon cher Canada,	My dear Canada,
Mon regard languissant	My longing glance
Vers toi se portera.	Will turn towards thee.

Sillery's parody may be roughly translated as:

A wandering Canadian,	To the fugitive current
Banished from his home,	He addressed these words:
Went wandering and fucking	
Through foreign bordellos.	If you just come as pee-pee,
	Oh warm seed from my loins,
One day, sad and thoughtful,	I'll turn into a queer.
Lying with an old bag,	One does what one can!

"Comprende?" inquired a Mexican. *"Va a explicar unas palabras de la cancion."* Sillery went on:

> *Si tu deviens pipi,*
> *O déduit chaleureux...*

"In the first place, one must not forget, ladies and gentlemen, that the poet resorts here to a trope analogous to prosopopoeia as he lends an autonomous life to..."

"I'll be hanged if I understand a goddamn word of what the guy is saying!" protested the same American voice.

"Sshh!"

"Shut up!"

Sillery went on. "So much for that. Now to go on with the terminology. The first term which, so to speak, is thrust at us goes by the name of *'pipi.'* Such a word, ladies and gentlemen, is quite difficult to comprehend. Although it escapes our grasp, it..."

"Que dice?"

"Nos de la significacion de 'pipi.'"

"But, let's not beat about the bush," continued Augustin. *"'Pipi':* masculine noun, watery substance, very much appreciated by the shipwrecked, so they say. *De gustibus non est disputandum.* And that..."

By this time, half the lights had been switched off. Closing time was near and Sillery's interruption threatened to slow down the drinking. "Last round, folks," the waiters started to shout, "closin' in a quarter of an hour."

Sillery came down from his perch, but not without a gesture of resignation. Young Langevin was holding his sides in laughter. "Really great, Augustin!"

Sillery inhaled deeply. His nostrils quivered. "You liked it? Really?"

"It was just fan-tas-tic!" Langevin's baby face was aglow with boundless admiration.

18

Augustin looked him over for a few seconds. "Maybe you think that it's easy for me," he said. Langevin shrugged as if he knew nothing of it. "Well, I'll tell you, it's real torture."

"Torture?"

"Yes. When I was young — I mean when I was younger, because I presume that even for you, I am not an old man..."

"You're just kidding."

"Seven years can be quite a lot sometimes. Although at eighteen I was far from being as worldly wise as you are." Langevin flushed with delight. "I've learned quite a few things since I've known you."

"Well, when I was young, I was terrified of crowds. I could hardly open my mouth, not even to say hello."

"No kidding?" Langevin did not seem very convinced nor very interested. Augustin had counted on making a greater impression.

"Anyway, I settled that problem in a jiffy."

"That figures."

"Here's how it happened. One day my cousin came over for a visit. She was a tall girl, thin and uptight, and about four or five years older than me. I pinched her bum quite hard in front of all the relatives. Naturally, she squawked and..." Sillery stopped right then and there. Langevin, head nodding and eyes half-closed, was about to pass out.

"Time to go bye-bye?" asked Augustin in a shrill tone. "Maybe you would like to go home?"

Langevin opened his eyes wide, trying to assume a hard look. "Back home? Hey, come on! I can stay up for three nights without a break."

Sillery pursed his lips, took a deep breath, and asked, "What do your parents say when you walk in at five o'clock in the morning, stinking of booze?"

19

Langevin pouted indifferently. "Nah! the ol'man just has his usual mouthing fit. It doesn't bother me."

"Your father a nice guy? Do you ever mention me to him?"

"He's so so. Middle class, bourgeois. I've probably brought up your name a couple of times at home. There's no love lost..."

"No? That's strange! And what do they say ?"

"Nonsense."

"Like?"

"Oh, I don't know... Like, for instance, they say it's because of you that I bum around."

"And what do you say then?"

"Nothing. I just let them go on yakking..."

The clapping of hands was heard once more in the hall. Sillery was startled and looked toward the stage. The "country nightingale," a heavy and stocky vocalist was throwing kisses to the audience. Lebeuf and Weston had resumed talking.

Still annoyed by Langevin's dozing, Sillery felt the urge to disturb their dialogue. "Don't tell me, gentlemen, that you still haven't settled the fate of Canada and French-Canadian letters. Although my little ditty must have been a valuable help to you!"

"It's coming," said Lebeuf. "A few more all-night sessions and we'll have cleared the approaches to the problem."

"Good, sirs, really good! I didn't know you were so close to your goal." He gave Langevin a poke with his elbow. "As I was explaining to this young man just the other day, the only reason my learned friend Lebeuf so assiduously frequents these dens of iniquity, of which La Bougrine is such a deplorable example, is to tap a surplus of inspiration suitable to nurture the masterpiece simmering in his skull."

"All right," said Lebeuf. "I never ask you how you spend your time. Everyone knows."

Sillery spread his arms in a grand gesture as if meaning to have others bear witness to Jules' ill will. "Okay, I didn't say anything. Let it pass. Though I was going to add that if you spent one hundredth of the energy you put into public ratiocination in writing, you... but I'll say no more... A voice clamoring in the desert. I would never dream of depriving you, even for the briefest time, of your little intellectual masturbation."

Lebeuf froze for an instant, his jaws tight. *He's gonna blow his top* thought Weston.

But the big man calmed down and shrugged his shoulders. "At least, I don't need others to masturbate me," he said.

"You two aren't going to fight over a matter of sperm, are you!" said Langevin, blushing.

Augustin burst into a sonorous laugh. "Don't you find, gentlemen, that this young man is making remarkable progress!"

Lebeuf uttered some sort of growl. "He talks about sperm more often than he used to, if that's what you mean."

Sillery squinted as if a spotlight were hurting his eyes. "Dear, oh dear! Do you want to know the difference between you and me?"

"It's not hard to find," said Lebeuf.

"The difference is that you always get on your intellectual high horse. You play the reformer; you're a nightclub Socrates. But, in fact, you lead exactly the same life as we do. Your daemon ought to whisper that to you from time to time."

"Enough," said Lebeuf, now annoyed. "Nobody asked you!"

Weston intervened. "Gentlemen, Socrates could drink

21

one amphora of wine after the other and continue his discussion in a completely philosophical manner. Now, I propose..."

He, in turn, was interrupted by the shouts of the waiters, who were now beginning to pick up the chairs. "It's time, fellows. We're closing."

The four companions drank up their whiskey in a hurry and left.

III

Lebeuf made up his mind to walk home. He wrapped his scarf around his neck, did up the zipper on his Canadian duffle coat, lit his pipe and set off. Dorchester Street was deserted, silent. The street lamps lined up their blinking bulbs as far as the eye could see. Dirty snow mixed with sand was spread in large patches over the sidewalk. Gusts of wind slapped against the awnings in front of pawnshops.

Jules shivered. He felt depressed. Sillery's remarks had stung him to the quick. *A nightclub Socrates — not a bad expression after all* he thought. *It's mostly when Langevin's around that he attacks me. He would do anything to impress that kid... But it shouldn't matter.*

Anyway, Lebeuf was not that concerned about Sillery's approval. The stories about an Oedipus complex and pederasty left him cold. But that wasn't the question.

The big man had to stop at a street corner as an almost empty streetcar came rattling and rocking down the tracks. Then he resumed his walk. His massive shadow swung in front of him, like a puppet. The question was not to know whether Sillery respected him or not, but whether Sillery was right in calling him a nightclub Socrates... He did waste a lot of time in cafes. All that drinking didn't lead anywhere. The next day he would stay in bed all morning, skip classes and not find the time to write. And Marguerite always made a scene every time he came home late. Marguerite! Lebeuf smiled a faint, dissillusioned smile. At first he had been foolish enough to believe that the arrangement would solve his problems. No more chasing after chicks, no more visits to the cathouse, a tidy, quiet and studious life. Cohabitation with the waitress had appeared to be the ideal solution.

And during the first months, Lebeuf had in fact tidied up his life. He went out only twice a week, the nights Marguerite was working. The rest of the time, he would read, make notes and write a little. Around eleven o'clock he would leave for his job at the Metropolitan Transport Company. In short, things were going fairly well. Even then, Lebeuf wrote very little — a few psychological notes, a short story of no value, which had ended up in the wastepaper basket.

Jules stopped and knocked out his pipe against the heel of his shoe. The tobacco fell in the snow with a slight crackling. Then he continued walking... The period of calm had not lasted for long. Margot had started to nag. "You don't take care of me enough. It's like being a dog," she had complained. Rows had become increasingly frequent. Lebeuf often sought some kind of refuge in the Saint Sulpice Library. He would walk in there fuming, his nerves on edge, and would sit down in an alcove determined to write. Write! Writing seemed to be the real, the only "solution." But as soon as he sat down the urge to smoke would take hold of him and not let up. He would madly scribble a paragraph or two, then would rush off for a few drags in the entrance hall. He would come back numbed and tormented by the thought of his weakness. He would read over what he had just written: thoughts, scenes for a novel, sometimes even short prose poems to keep his hand in. It all seemed uniformly insipid, inconsistent and amateurish improvisation. *If only we had the right to smoke in this library...* He had started going out again, had made friends with Weston, and now he frequented nightclubs almost every night. Afterwards, except on his days off, he rushed to work, knocked off his eight hours (from midnight to eight), then sometimes made it to the university, sometimes trudged back to his room to fall asleep. It was not much of a life.

Lebeuf was now walking along the Champs de Mars. He hunched slightly forward to brace himself against the wind and rubbed his ears. At the top of the slope, to the right, the hulking gray shape of the City Hall stood out, capped by its Renaissance lantern. Jules then crossed the street and walked close to the rough concrete wall of the Armoury to protect himself against the wind. He was still brooding over the same dark thoughts. Margot was responsible for this situation. It was her constant nagging that forced his nocturnal wanderings. Otherwise he would be writing. He always worked best at night. Now all his nights were lost. Marguerite was there like a bloodsucker, draining off his energy, his peace of mind. *I've gotta dump her. It's been going on for too long* he had repeated to himself at least once a week in the last five months.

The big man reached Saint Denis Street. Across from him, the tall oaks of Viger Square stood in line along the paths, waving their naked branches in the half-light. To the left, high on his pedestal, Doctor Chenier was urging the patriots to fight. Two cabs, their dome lights on, passed by with a rubbery hiss. Lebeuf sought shelter behind a newsstand to light his pipe, after which he went on walking toward Saint Luc Hospital. *Anyway, one way or the other, it has to change.* What could be more absurd than the life he was leading? And for so long! Started working at fifteen as a delivery boy, emigrated to his uncle's place in Boston to work in the textile mills, returned to Canada to start his *cours classique** at twenty. Then the university, faculty of humanities courses that bored him and which he paid for by slaving as a clean-up man at the Transport Company. And what was it all for? What were the results? He was twenty-nine. He was a sweeper. And what afterwards? Once he had his honors degree, would he be better off?

"You wouldn't have any spare change, mister, for a poor old man who's hungry?" A toothless vagrant smelling of alcohol stood before him, hat in hand.

Lebeuf went through his pockets. "I never refused anybody a drink. Here's fifty cents, Pop. Have fun."

"God bless..."

"Forget it."

Jules quickened his pace. He crossed Sainte Catherine Street, walked along in front of L'école Polytechnique.

---

*Until the late 1950s, the traditional *cours classique* was the backbone of higher education in French Canada. Given in the Church-supported *collèges,* it was a strict, classical education, stressing the liberal arts and Thomistic philosophy. Spanning what would be the period of both secondary and undergraduate education under the English system, the course lasted either six or eight years, the former leading to a B.L. certificate, the latter to a B.A. Students who completed their degree could continue as graduate students at the universities, almost always under the Faculties of Arts, Medicine, or Law — the only areas for which they were prepared — unless they chose the priesthood.

Because the *collèges* charged tuition and were geared to full-time study, students came mostly from the upper and middle classes, although the Church could be counted on to provide help for poor but outstanding students. The usual age of entrance was 13 or 14 (after Grade 6 of the Church-run primary schools).

The *collèges* admitted boys only. Girls seeking higher education were accommodated in private (often boarding) schools, usually under convent auspices, which offered studies more or less equivalent to the *cours classique.*

On the right, the pointed steeple of Saint Jacques' penetrated the dark sky. Then he stopped in front of a bookshop window. A new Simenon novel was on display. Lebeuf gazed dreamily at the novelist's picture: pipe in mouth, slouch hat, piercing self-assured look... *That's probably his two hundredth book,* he mused. To write readable novels, capable of captivating a reader throughout a whole evening — Lebeuf could ask for nothing more for the time being. That would at least be a start. He absent-mindedly ran his hand through his reddish brush-cut. *I'll never make it, I haven't got the imagination; I'll never produce anything but serious novels. A half-ass Bazin or Bourget.* Yet, a slight hope still simmered deep within him. *You never know, maybe I have some talent.* The thing was, he would have to really work at it.

Quickening his pace, he passed the Saint Sulpice Library and arrived home — a rooming house made of gray stones, blackened by soot. Above the entrance a green awning on the wrought-iron canopy formed a cloth dome. White and yellow aluminum ''koolvents'' jutted over the windows. With a quick glance, the student made sure that no light filtered through the shutters of his second-floor bedroom window. *She must be asleep.* He proceeded to walk up the stairs. A vague, musty smell lingered throughout the building. At first, he had liked the smell. He had associated it with a feeling of comfort and security. Now he detested it. The steps groaned under his feet. It was enough to wake up the dead, he reflected.

At his entrance, he carefully turned the key, pushed the door open, cocked an ear toward the darkness. Nothing. He could hear Marguerite breathing. *She is not asleep, she's waiting for me.* The thought filled him with rage. Resolutely he flipped the switch on. A stark light flooded the room, like a liquid. Sitting up in the bed, arms crossed over her chest, Margot stared at him with blinking eyes.

Her narrow forehead, her slightly turned-up nose between round, full cheeks jarred with her stiff posture and tight-lipped mouth.

"Hello," said Lebeuf. "Everything okay?"

Marguerite started to bite her lips without answering.

True, I'd promised to take her out to the movies last night, thought Lebeuf. As if nothing had happened, he walked over to the mirror and had a look at himself. His eyes were burning and his mouth was coated. *Things have got to change.* He slouched down in a chair and started to undress.

"Some people think 'cause you gotta work in a restaurant and they go to university, they think you're not so smart, it looks like." Her angry voice tripped on syllables. Lebeuf shrugged and walked over to the sink.

"Some think that way, but if that's what they think then they're off the track. If they think that just 'cause you work in a restaurant, you can't figure things out, they're way way off the track. That's all I can say!"

Jules fastidiously placed the toothbrush and toothpaste back in the medicine cabinet. With his foot, he shoved aside a pile of clothes that were lying on the floor.

"I've never reproached you for working in a restaurant," he said. "That's where I met you."

Quickly unfolding her fleshy arms, Margot slammed both hands down on the mattress. "Well that takes the cake! Blame me for working in a restaurant! That really takes the cake! 'Cause you work in a restaurant doesn't mean you're stupider than the next one. But Gentleman Joe here thinks he's better. Gentleman Joe goes to university. He says he wants to be a writer."

Margot paused briefly looking for new sarcastic quips. "Writing! Writing what? Just ask me! I disturb him. The gentleman is disturbed when I'm here! He can't work! So meanwhile, he spends his time hanging around nightclubs with his buddies. And me, in the meantime, I twiddle my thumbs like a damned fool, alone in this room!''

''I had matters to discuss,'' said Lebeuf.

'' 'Matters to discuss!' 'Matters to discuss!' What matters to discuss? But you got nothing to discuss with me, eh? You used to have enough things to discuss when you wanted to get me! Now, it doesn't matter any more.'' Lebeuf raised his hand meaning to interrupt her, but she went on. ''Some people think you're not good enough 'cause you don't go to university. They think you don't understand nothing... Well in the first place, what were you discussing? Tell me.''

Lebeuf made a vague lazy gesture. ''It wouldn't interest you. Piles of stuff. We talked about language, the Quebec attitude... I don't know...''

Marguerite pinched her lips trying to imitate her lover's intonation: '' 'We talked about the Quebec attitude.' That's just like you all right! You spend your time spitting on the Québécois.''

Lebeuf wheeled around completely. ''That's not true!''

Margot's anger flared to a heightened violence. ''You come and say that that's not true to me? 'Québécois don't speak proper, Québécois don't read books. Québécois do this, Québécois do that.' To your mind, the Québécois never do a damned thing right.''

Lebeuf shrugged. What was the use of arguing? Marguerite would not understand. He should never have brought up the question in front of her.

''Besides, what do you think you are? You're not a Québécois like everybody else? You're not one, eh? You think you're smarter than everybody else 'cause you go to university, but if you're so smart how come you have to clean shit from streetcars? Eh? How come you're a shit cleaner, if you're so smart?''

Lebeuf gave her a stunned look. It was the first time she

had fought him on that territory. Lebeuf boasted in front of other students about his "realistic" job. "Shut up! he said. "You're going berserk. A minute ago, I was supposed to sniff at waitresses 'cause I was a university student. Now you blame me for being a sweeper."

"I don't blame you for bein' a sweeper," she replied in a calmer tone. "You know that damned well. There's got to be sweepers just like there's got to be waitresses. But you can't be two things at once. You can't sit on the fence. When you don't have enough money to go to university, well, you just do what you can do. You start at the bottom and try to better yourself, that's all. If you wanted to be a doctor or a lawyer, I wouldn't say so much. But what the hell is it you want to be? I've never been able to get it out of you."

She waited a few moments for an answer that did not come, then lay on her back with a sigh. Lebeuf spread his pants over the back of a chair, turned off the overhead light and also slipped between the sheets. His head was spinning slightly. His tongue felt as rough as a grate. *It's gotta change*. After all, Margot wasn't wrong. What sort of double life was this? If he had stayed in Boston, he would have been settled down by now, established... Jules rolled over heavily in his bed. A ray of light filtered in through the shutters and fell on a pile of dirty clothes that lay on the floor. A streetcar went moaning by. Marguerite was motionless. Why had he come back to Montreal? Montreal was not that different from Boston... Of course Jules had not understood the Americans. But could he understand better here? The university on one side, the sweepers on the other. Between the two, a wide range of social classes. Topping off the whole thing, two ethnic groups, with different ways of thinking and different languages. Lebeuf himself belonged to one of these groups... He dug his head into his pillow, seeking a

30

comfortable position. It was this whole complexity that needed to be expressed in a novel. Bring Montreal to life, give it a soul of some kind. Another streetcar rattled by on Saint Denis Street. Must be three-forty, he thought. Marguerite had fallen asleep. She snored lightly at his side. Jules took her in his arms. She uttered a weak moan. *At least there's this. That's one thing certain.*

IV

Stepping out of the cab, Sillery thought he saw the silhouette of a man standing in a doorway a few houses from his home. He instantly forgot Langevin's "revolting" behavior and leaned forward to have a better look at the doorway in the distant light and shade. It was hard to see clearly because of shadows of branches that swept the façade of the house. Augustin could not make out anything. But the man might have pulled back to hide in the porch. *What in the world could he want?* He froze on the spot, his heart pounding. Throughout his childhood he had been afraid of unlit rooms, closets, dark streets. His mother had to look under his bed, in the wardrobes, even in the drawers before tucking him in to bed. *It's another illusion like the ones I used to have when I was little.* But he wasn't reassured. He remained motionless in front of the door for a few seconds, staring in the direction of the apparition. *I'm a perfect target. I should go in.* But he lingered a while longer, shaking. Was it fear? A fascination with danger? Sillery tried to gather his thoughts. Who could be after him? No one at all, nobody. Was that certain? Sodomites often unwittingly stir up inexorable hatred around themselves. What if people had found out about his affair with René? *Precisely — my last note wasn't answered.* For a while he had seen the young student every day. But for some time now, René had been acting rather reluctant, standing him up, making up vague excuses to get away. Fortunately, Augustin himself had become tired of the boorish and scruffy teenager, who had limited intelligence. He was much more fascinated by Langevin . . . Suddenly, his thoughts moved back to the apparition. *I should go and see if there's really someone there*. But he knew he would do nothing. At best he could barely face his enemy by remaining frozen at a distance. Finally, he took a deep breath and inserted the key in the lock.

"Is that you, Augustin?"

"Yes, mother, it's me."

His mother never reprimanded him for any reason. When he didn't come home by the wee hours of the morning, she would merely get up earlier than usual and wait for him in the dining room, sipping a brew of green tea and chicory.

The dining-room door was ajar. Sillery noticed his mother, immobile, faintly visible in the weak light of the candle, a steaming cup in her hand. That primitive lighting, which she preferred to anything else, clashed with the rich furniture displayed about the room. In the half-light could be seen two carved oak cabinets, china what-nots and a few paintings.

"Shall I turn on the light?"

Mrs. Sillery gestured apprehensively. "No, no, it's not worth the trouble."

She spoke with a solemn voice, slightly weary. Despite the early hour — it was barely five o'clock — she was fully dressed. Her gray hair, neatly gathered at the back in an old-fashioned bun, accentuated her high, wrinkle-free forehead.

"What are you going to have?"

Augustin knew there was no point in refusing. "Whatever you wish. Toast and coffee..."

Mrs. Sillery got up and went into the kitchen.

I've got to work on Pascal today reflected Augustin. Two months before, he had begun rereading *Les Pensées* for an essay required in his course on the seventeenth century. This essay, entitled "The Rhetoric of Pascal," had been in the professor's hands for several weeks now, but Sillery continued to delve into his subject. Which parts of *Les Pensées* and *Les Provinciales* appealed to the intelligence, which to the imagination — that was the question. *After all it's stupid. Neither intelligence nor imagination exist, they are old outdated concepts.* Yet, he still went on researching the subject. For the purpose of analysis, it was legitimate to establish certain distinctions. Was it reasons of the mind or reasons of the heart that had made Pascal himself bow to conversion? Why does one become a convert? Why does one lose one's faith? Unanswerable questions, like all the questions which are truly important...

"Coffee?"

"Yes, thank you, mother."

Despite his doubts, Sillery remained confident that his research would bear fruit. For the first time he was working methodically. He jotted down on individual index cards the "intellectual" passages, the "imaginative," the "emotional" and the "doubtful." He even had subdivided the "emotional" into three groups — "fear," "love," "shame." *It isn't satisfactory; I'll have to break it down even more.*

"I've made poached eggs for you. And I've found some Gruyère cheese." Mrs. Sillery placed all the food in front of her son.

"Thank you." He started to eat and discovered that he was hungry. There was a moment of silence.

"Madeleine spent the evening here yesterday," said Mrs. Sillery.

Augustin knew why his mother had mentioned

Madeleine's name. For a long time now, she had been wanting him to marry the girl. But she never broached the subject directly.

"Did she play the piano?"

"Only two pieces."

"She's talented..."

"Yes, she is talented."

"Especially with Debussy," he said after a pause. "Chopin too, but especially Debussy. She is more at ease with the impressionistic mode. She is not romantic at all..." *Another trite comment* he thought.

"There's always something romantic about a young woman... because you see..." Mrs. Sillery got up. "Shall I pour you another cup?" She tilted the percolator.

"What were you saying about romanticism?" asked Augustin.

"Nothing. I don't believe in generalizations anymore..."

A sudden slamming of a door startled them both. Quick, heavy steps were heard in the hall.

"Can't a person even sleep in this house, for Christ's sake?"

Paunchy, broad-backed, red-faced and dishevelled, Mr. Sillery came into the dining room in his pin-striped robe, gesticulating.

"Is this a madhouse here? You sleep all day and stay up all night?" The bursts of his strong voice seemed to spur him on. "But while you two are lounging around the house, I'm the one who has to work..."

Augustin frowned at his father's peremptory interruption, while Mrs. Sillery, elbows on the table, stared blankly.

This reception did not cool Mr. Sillery's verve. Did they take him for a moron? They lived a life of sybarites, while he had to... He ran out of words to express how he felt. His cheeks swelled and he uttered a sort of hiss. What work did he have to do? "Maybe you don't know what I have to do? Well I'll tell you!" At least once a week, he felt the need to shake them out of their ignorance. "I get up at a decent hour, I do! I don't spend my time daydreaming all night or gadding about the town's nightclubs!" No, he had to work like a horse, adding up rows of digits, purchasing, selling, keeping an eye on the market, always on the lookout. And what was his son doing all that time? "He was weighing flies' feet on cobweb scales."

"On cobweb scales!" he repeated, pleased with the quotation. But for Christ's sake! It wasn't going to go on. He was going to clamp down. He would have the last laugh.

Augustin cast a furtive glance at his mother. Elbows on the table, motionless, she was staring blankly. *When will she ever answer back?* wondered Augustin. He himself became completely disconcerted whenever he had to face his father.

Mr. Sillery stopped a while in order to catch his breath. His wife came out of her daze to say in a calm voice. "You should be happy today, Georges."

"Happy? What do you mean, happy." Mr. Sillery was flailing his arms as Augustin watched him out of the corner of his eye.

"Of course," replied his wife. "Happy to have found a pretext to exercise your vocal cords so early."

"Vocal cords!" spewed out Mr. Sillery.

Was he not the master of his own house? Did they expect to prevent him from talking in his own house?

Mrs. Sillery let him finish, then said, "Yes, you should be happy. You need your little vocal exercise daily and since you lack the imagination to find new excuses you usually end up straining your brain."

That remark sent the businessman to new heights of

rage. "Excuses! You call that an excuse!" That went too far! His patience had reached the breaking point. He would go and live elsewhere. How could things like this happen? Being awakened at five in the morning by two maniacs who stayed up all night gabbing and fiddling around by candlelight. Candlelight! The idea struck him. He had forgotten, He rushed over and angrily flipped the switch.

Augustin got up without looking at his father. "If you'll excuse me, mother, I'll retire to my room." He kissed his mother's forehead and, with his head held high, walked by Mr. Sillery. *Such vulgarity must not keep me from my work* he thought.

As always his room was impeccably tidy. Mahogany desk in the center; oak shelves mounted on yellow and green bricks along two walls; a portrait of Pascal; a Voltaire armchair, the only antique in the place.

To be alone in a room. Sillery felt extremely tense. He took a few deep breaths, raising his arms. *I must work anyway.* He took off his rust-colored jacket and placed it on a hanger. There was a stain on the left sleeve. Beer or whiskey? He sniffed it. It did not smell of anything. He hung the jacket in the wardrobe and started pacing the room. *I've got to work.* He sat at his desk, took out his index cards and absent-mindedly thumbed through them. Imagination, intelligence, emotion, divisions, subdivisions — all nonsense.

Unable to concentrate, he pushed the cards away and started to fidget in his chair. He had the urge to rush to the window to see if the man was really there. No. It was childish. He wouldn't give in. He wiped his moist hands with a handkerchief and made himself read a few paragraphs. *I will not give in.* Then suddenly he darted to the window and scrutinized the pale dawn. *Nobody. I knew it* he said as beads of sweat glistened on his forehead. *I knew it, but I gave in just the same.* He stepped back to his desk, head bowed, and began to scan through his cards. *I gave in just the same.* In a sudden flare of temper, he closed his folder. *No use trying. I won't be able to work today.* His heart was beating madly.

V

At a street corner, Weston stepped on a patch of ice. It gave a sharp crack and water splashed up to his ankle, filling his shoe. He uttered a curse. *I'll hafta buy snowboots.* That's what he had been saying all winter long. Now, spring was not far off; what was the use. In St. Louis the trees were blooming by now. In Paris, too, no doubt. "Damn weather," he mumbled to himself. "Here we are in March and still snowbound. How can people stand it?"

Yet Weston did not regret coming to Montreal. He might have done worse. Before leaving St. Louis, a guy had told him that all French Canadians were uncouth farmers. The newly arrived ex-G.I. had first come upon Sillery! A few days later he met up with Lebeuf. On the whole, he couldn't complain. He stopped for a while and pressed his foot down against the ground. There was a swishing inside his shoe, but it wasn't as cold now. Ken went on walking. The whiskey he had drunk at La Bougrine still made him warm all over. He started recalling the evening's discussion. Especially he remembered Jules' fury at Sillery's digs. *A funny guy, that Lebeuf,* he thought. *Although usually calm, any allusion to his literary endeavors makes him go right off the deep end.* In a way Ken could understand that. His own thesis on French Canadians were driving him up the wall. But it wasn't the same. His thesis was not of prime importance to him, whereas for Lebeuf, you would swear that his whole life depended on it. *A real funny guy*.

Weston began reconsidering the difficulties involved with his thesis. *Statistics vs life* he mused. How could the two be reconciled? How could you fuse these two opposite poles in the form of a thesis on French Canadians? Ken had the impression that his most interesting experiences in Montreal had nothing to do with his work. Statistics, documents on one side; life on the other. Between the two, an abyss. He knew what he should have done. He should have gone into the Quebec countryside and observed, as Louis Hémon had done. Otherwise, it would have been just as well to stay in St. Louis and write his thesis from the documents.

Weston walked a little farther, head bowed, wrapped in his thoughts. The street lamps had just gone off. Far ahead, in the pale dawn, the saw-toothed skyline of the riverside was slowly emerging from the darkness. A milk cart trundled past, pulled by a huge, reddish horse, trotting. *Why did I let anyone stick me with such a topic?* Yet that was not quite right. The only interesting guy on the faculty, to Weston's mind, had been the history and sociology professor. He had gone to see him and had talked his thesis subject over with him. The professor had suggested the French Canadians as a topic, and Ken had agreed right away. *That'll be easy. All I'll have to do is open my eyes and observe* he had thought at the time. *How naive!* He didn't know what a mess he would become involved in.

I might just as well be blind; none of my personal connections are of any use to me. Weston kicked at an ice pebble sticking out in the middle of the sidewalk. He lit a cigarette. No, it was not right to assume that none of his connections was useful. What about Thérèse? If you forgot about her old-maid idiosyncracies, which were the same everywhere, then what was left was probably genuine French Canadian. And yet, how could he really be sure?

Ken stepped up his pace. He felt the urge to get home now. Thérèse would surely be up already. She was up at six to get the other roomers' breakfast, bring in the milk, help her mother get dressed. Weston smiled. *Maybe she also likes to be there when I roll in.*

During the first days of his stay in Montreal, the American had had quite a few chats with Thérèse. Feeling lost, not knowing anybody and wanting to learn French, he had spent whole evenings talking with her. Then he had met Lebeuf and had started to go out. Of course, Thérèse felt a little sore over the desertion, but what could he do? Ken felt sorry for her. What a life — looking after her sick mother, preparing meals, making beds, cleaning house. The poor girl had a raw deal. And she wasn't very pretty on top of it all. How was it he had thought of courting her? When you're new in a place, you're after all the girls. It had been the same with Montreal at the beginning; everything had seemed so picturesque, so quaint. Now almost nothing was left of those impressions — only a few notes on a pad. Weston felt the need to go over things, straighten them out in his mind. French Canadians were generally shorter than Americans. Their hair was darker and a few had moustaches. There were many churches in Montreal, most of them Catholic. The streetcars were slow. People jostled one another to cram into them; they seemed to be lacking in civic-mindedness. Traffic in the downtown area was absolutely impossible. But the city itself was reasonably clean, cleaner than cities in America, though not as clean as cities in England. French-Canadian girls, also on the short side, were smart dressers. Often they had generous breasts and hips which made them very desirable. What else? The old quarter by

41

the river, around Place d'Armes and the Bonsecours Market, had a certain charm. The mountain, of course, gave the city its distinctive attractiveness. And then — the most important thing, of course — the mixture of English and French, and the incomprehensible pig-headedness of the English in refusing to learn to speak French. The influence of the Catholic clergy? Hard to define. A considerable influence, apparently, but there was a more or less silent resistance. Ken had not been able to make up his mind about that.

All in all, it seemed like a lot. There was material for quite an interesting article in some big American magazine. But a thesis? That remained to be seen...

Weston's room was on the ground floor, near the kitchen. He had hoped to sneak in unnoticed. But just as he entered, Thérèse showed up at the kitchen door. Her thin lips were compressed in a nervous smile. "Well, well. The night hawks are coming back to the nest!"

Such artificial language annoyed Weston. But what could he do about it?

"The early birds are up too, I see," he said, hating himself for falling into the same manner of speaking.

"Did the night hawks catch any innocent doves last night?"

Ken shrugged. "Women always imagine that when a guy goes out at night it's always for a bash."

"*Imagine?* Well, yes, I guess we do. It's awful to think how perverted *our* imagination can be!" Standing opposite him in her long apron of a mauve flower-print, she smiled her crooked smile. "But it's you, the night hawks, that are responsible. You're the ones that make us imagine all those things."

"I hope you're not losing any sleep over it." Speaking in French, he had said *"j'espère ça ne..."*

' *"J'espère que,'* " corrected Thérèse.

42

' "*Que*', '*que*', '*que*,' " repeated Weston in an irritated tone.

"What's this! Getting angry with your teacher now? Somebody must have had a bad night."

Ken was fuming. If only she could overlook a mistake or two once in a while. It was an obsession with her.

"Would anyone like a cup of coffee to help recover?"

"All right," he said, in English this time.

Weston stepped into the kitchen. Both cups were already on the table, along with the cream and sugar. A percolator was steaming on the low burner. Thérèse dug a spoon into the sugar.

"One, two, that's it?"

"Yes."

The old maid sat across from him and gave him a protective look. She had rather attractive, sea-green eyes. If only she would use a little makeup! Her complexion was grayish.

"Now, are you going to tell your teacher what you did last night?"

"There's nothing to tell."

"Ah! Somebody wants to keep his little secrets."

"There are no secrets. We went over to the Blue Sky, then on to La Bougrine. We had a few drinks. We talked about things. Sillery came out with an obscene song... That's all."

Thérèse had seemingly lost her composure. "An obscene song, Sillery?"

Augustin had been over twice to see Ken. The old maid had been impressed by his good manners and his polished speech. How could he? An obscene song? Well, now!

"What sort of song?"

"I can't remember the words."

Again Weston made an error in French, saying "*des mots*" instead of "*les mots*."

" 'Les mots,' " Thérèse corrected.

"Okay, 'les mots.' I don't remember them. If you like, next time he's around, I'll ask him to teach you the words."

"The words do not interest me one bit, I assure you."

"All right then, I won't ask him."

They sipped their coffee and remained silent for a while. Ken gazed at the old maid's tired-looking, sallowish complexion and veined hands. Suddenly he asked, "Thérèse, how come you never go out?"

"Go out? But I go out to the movies now and then."

"No, I mean..."

"You mean, go out the way you do?"

"Yes. Go to a cafe once in a while, meet people..."

"You want to take me out, is that it?"

Weston ran his palm over his chin. Maybe he should have kept his mouth shut.

"La Bougrine?" asked Thérèse "No, I couldn't. You know that I have to look after mama."

"Why?" Ken caught himself asking. "Mrs. Beauchamp is quite capable of looking after herself for one evening!"

Thérèse warned him with a silencing gesture.

"She puts on an act just to keep you home," whispered Weston. "You can't — how do you say..." He searched for the French equivalent of "waste your life." Finally, he came up with "gaspiller votre vie."

"Yes, I understand. I understand very well. You don't want to go out with me, an ex-G.I." Why had he said that? He knew it wasn't true.

"You're being unfair, Ken. You..."

She stopped and listened. Weston did too. They heard the opening of a door and Mrs. Beauchamp dragging her feet down the hall.

"Thérèse, Thérèse," called a whining voice. "Is

44

breakfast ready? It's six-thirty. Who's in there with you? What are you doing."

"I'm having a cup of coffee," Thérèse shouted back. "With Kenneth."

Mrs. Beauchamp made her appearance. She was a big, pink-skinned old lady with a fallen-in mouth and small piercing eyes under bushy eyebrows.

"Oh! Ken is here!" she said without looking at him. "I thought he was out."

Weston got up. "I've got to work. Good-bye. We'll talk about it some other time."

Thérèse answered him with a nod of her head.

VI

Lebeuf opened the door of the "shack." It was an oblong room, approximately twenty-five by eight feet, furnished with wooden benches. Two windows protected by wire netting were on each side of the room. Light glared from a naked bulb hanging from the ceiling onto a huge table scarred by knife cuts in the center of the room. The shack stood behind the main office, Hochelaga section, of the Montreal Metropolitan Transport Company. A wicket linked the shack to the booth of the cashier, a big paunchy man, completely bald, who sporadically stuck out his head like a jack-in-the-box in order to take part in the conversation.

When Lebeuf walked into the shack, a single sweeper was there, sitting at the other end of the room, chewing away at a sandwich. He was a small toothless man in his forties, with mousy eyes, thin, dish-water hair and a protruding chin. He was known as Bill, a diminutive with no apparent relationship to his real name, Phillipe Lafrenière.

It was three-thirty in the morning, "lunch time." In fact, the company gave no time off for lunch. A "day's work" for the night cleaning crew officially lasted from midnight to eight, nonstop. But there was an unspoken agreement between the employees and the management. The foreman was always absent at "lunch time"; it was only fair, thought the sweepers, considering the nuisance of having to work at night.

"Hey there, Lebeuf," mumbled Bill, his mouth full.

"Hey, Bill."

"Everythin' awright?" Even with nothing in his mouth, Bill spoke with a sort of chopping sound, as if his tongue was forever swimming in a pool of saliva.

"Yeah, everythin' okay." Jules dropped heavily to the bench. He felt tired. *Two hours' sleep a night is not enough. I'll have to get myself a really good night's sleep one of these nights.*

"Any tar in yer cars, Lebeuf?"

"No."

"Well, yuh just wouldn't believe what I got. It won't come off. Yuh could wear out yer hands right up to the elbows, and Christ, it still wouldn't come off!"

"Yeah, well, we'll go over and give you a hand there in a minute." Lebeuf opened his lunchpail and put his thermos down on the table.

"Hi there, boys."

"Well, here's Bouboule."

Bouboule — Onésime Boulé was his real name — was a sad-faced, dull-eyed old man in his sixties. With his long swinging arms and his shaky gait, he looked like a sleepwalker. An enormous Adam's apple moved constantly beneath his chin. But for all his phlegmatic appearance, the soul of a revolutionary fumed in Bouboule. He nurtured a ferocious hatred for big wheels in general and for the Transport Company in particular, and the threats he would pour forth against them in his calm little voice, without a gesture or flutter, were violent enough to make a communist swoon with delight.

As he had overheard Bill's remark about the tar, he was quick to add, "Just remember what I say, Bill. The way things are goin', they'll be fillin' them cars full o' shit and then asking us to lick'em clean. Hell! Tar gets into the wood and sets in deep, like yuh wouldn't believe. And then first thing yuh know that bitching brown-noser, Lévêque, comes around to tell yuh they're not clean enough. A shithead like that ought to be put through the friggin' meat grinder.''

As he was talking in his calm, small voice, Bouboule had gently opened his lunchpail and was carefully placing his sandwiches in front of him.

"Just remember what I tell yuh," he continued. "The way things are goin', they'll be filling our cars with shit!''

"Yeah!" said Lebeuf, "well you're not gonna tell me that the company spends its time throwing tar in the streetcars just for the fun of it.''

"They're capable of it," grumbled Bouboule, "it wouldn't surprise me a bit. They could, easily.''

"Listen," interrupted Bill, who had finally managed to finish one of his sandwiches. "Listen eh, Lebeuf, sometimes yuh talk to the inspector, don't yuh? Well, is it true that maybe we're really gonna go on strike?''

New sweepers walked in from time to time and sat down on the benches. Bouboule stopped eating. "We're gonna go on strike?''

"That's what I read in part of a newspaper I found lying around," explained Bill. "Apparently things are getting hot.''

"Really! You mean you read newspapers now? I thought your old man never showed you how to read!'' It was the cashier, who had just thrust his big, bald head through his wicket.

Loud guffaws from all sides followed the quip. It was well known that Bill's sons — all four of them — constantly played hooky from school.

In a fit of rage, Bill smashed his fist on the table top. "Christ! Don't you start with that again.''

"Are we going to strike?" asked Bouboule, staring at Lebeuf.

48

"It could be."

Curiosity was heightened.

"Are yuh sure?"

"When would it be for?"

"It would be in September, when the new contract is due in," said Jules.

"We're gonna strike for real?" repeated Bouboule, who had forgotten all about eating. "You mean, we're gonna be able to cream those goddamn lousy sons o' bitches?"

"I didn't say yes and I didn't say no," answered Lebeuf. "Anyway, it's none of my business."

His answer created a chill; September was far off yet. The sweepers, for the most part, had no money saved, but they would have gone on strike on the spot just to prove that they could do it.

"We all know you don't give a damn, Lebeuf. You go to university. It's none of your business," remarked Charlot, a small, bearded, gorilla-faced Italian.

"Christ, Charlot, don't you go and say a thing like that," protested Bill. "Don't say that! When they wanted us to shovel snow last winter, was it you or Lebeuf that went to the boss to protest? You, you were shittin' in yer pants for chrissake!"

"Maybe, maybe," admitted Charlot with a grimace. "But no matter what you say, Lebeuf and us are horses of a different color. That guy goes to university."

"I'm the same as you," answered Lebeuf. "I'm here to earn a living. It costs a few bucks to go to university, don't forget that."

"It costs a lot, the university?" asked Bill. "I know it's not my business to ask yuh about it, but my daughter, yuh know, well, she would like to go to a private convent school next year. She's sixteen now, you see. Well, do yuh know how much the nuns are asking?" Bill paused

49

for a moment. "They're askin' twenty-two bucks a month, not a cent less."

"Somebody in the family wantin' to learn how to read?" inquired the cashier, whose head reappeared through the wicket.

The sweepers shook with loud laughter again. Parizeau was in fine fettle today.

Bill was flushed with rage. "Zozo, I'm warning yuh! Yuh better get back into yer cage, yuh goddamn monkey. No way anybody can talk serious with that asshole around."

There was a pause and the chewing of the sandwiches could be heard. Finally Charlot spoke. "So, then it does cost a lot to go to university?"

Lebeuf hesitated. Should he tell the truth? He thought of Margot, who constantly stormed about his tuition fees. "It's about three hundred tomatoes a year," he announced finally.

Bill's eyes beamed wide with surprise. "Goddamn!"

"Goddamn sons of bitches of big shots," interrupted Bouboule in his meek voice.

Even Charlot's jaw dropped at the mention of such an astronomical sum.

"I'm not lucky enough to be a veteran," explained Jules.

"A veteran?" asked Bill. "How much do veterans have to pay?"

"They don't have to pay."

"They don't pay?"

"No. Far from it. They get something like ninety-five bucks, I think, on top of what they get to cover their fees. That's what bachelors get. If you're married it can go to a hundred and forty-five."

Bill almost choked. "Holy Jesus! Now we've seen everything. People get paid to go to school! Those are the

50

bloody gimmicks we end up having to pay taxes for."

"The money could be spent worse," said Lebeuf. "Billions were doled out for arms..."

"Goddamn sons of bitches of monopolizers," sententiously articulated Bouboule, not knowing exactly to whom he was referring. "They're always against the poor people! But Lebeuf, hell, why do you give those bastards three hundred dollars? You're workin' with us and everythin', why do you dish out three hundred beauties a year?"

Lebeuf made a vague gesture. How could he explain that to them? And yet did he really know for sure why he went to university?

Charlot took the occasion to throw in his word. "He's workin' with us and that's fine. But as I was saying a while back, he's a horse of a different color."

The student turned expressionless eyes toward him. The unshaded lightbulb caught the tawny hues of his brush-cut. "What do you mean, Charlot? I do my job."

"You do your job all right. I don't deny that. But still and all it's not the same thing. It's more like you're a tourist around here."

Charlot elbowed the man next to him, a big placid sweeper with wiggly jowls, who nodded his head in approval without interrupting his chewing.

"I'm no more a tourist than you are," said Jules. "I'm part of the gang."

The Italian threw his arms up in scepticism.

Bill, for his part, had not yet gotten over the scholarships allotted to veterans. "Just think of it. Christ! Ninety-five bucks a month, boys! That's a helluva lot o' bottles of beer, eh!"

"Those goddamn sons of bitches of monopolizers," said Bouboule, shaking his bald head.

Charlot was no longer following the conversation.

51

After a glance at the clock, he stuck his nose against one of the wire-netted windows.

"Watch it, boys. I can see Lévêque's lamp. He's coming over this way. We better beat it."

The sweepers got up grumbling.

"Hell!" said Bouboule, "no time to eat anymore?" He had been so engrossed in the conversation that he had finished only half his sandwiches. "Those bastards want to starve us to death now? It's not enough for us to have to clean their damn shit, now they want us to die like dogs."

"Don't stay here Bouboule. He's liable to report you."

Bouboule turned pale with rage. "Let 'im report me, hell, let 'im do it! A damn arsekisser like that's not gonna stop me from eating! Bouboule wasn't born yesterday." He stayed put on his bench, looking stubborn, as the other sweepers scurried off through the back door.

VII

Once outside, Bill grabbed Lebeuf's arm and pulled him towards the car barns. "Listen, Lebeuf, I got somethin', a little favor to ask yuh."

"Shoot."

Bill scratched his head with an air of perplexity. "Well, you see, it's like this. I told yuh back there that my girl — Gisèle's her name — well she'd like to go on studying in the fall. Christ, studies ain't my line, yuh see. But the ol' lady don't think like me. And like they say, it's not just 'cause she's my own kid, but she's got somethin' upstairs. My boys are dumbbells, I'm not afraid to say it, they're knucklebrains. Playing stupid tricks, breaking windows, acting smart, that's all they're good for. But studying..."

He glanced at Lebeuf to get his reaction. Jules shrugged.

"But Gisèle," he continued, "she's not like that. She learns quicker'n anybody. Pages and pages. Champlain, Joan of Arc, Moses, Colborne and that goddamn English; she can recite you it all off without a hitch." Sniffling, Bill ran his hand under his nose. It was not like him to make such long speeches. "So the ol' lady paid a visit to the parish priest with Gisèle last week. It looks like they jabbered for quite a while. So finally, according to the priest, we should allow her to go on..."

"Yeah? So?"

Bill scratched his head once more. "I got nothin'

against priests, me. Get that straight. They got their business to do and I got mine. I got nothin' against 'em. Only... well listen... if they want her to go on, then I figure I know why.''

"Why?''

"Why? It's clear and simple! Bill wasn't born yesterday. I tell yuh, they wanna make a nun outa her.''

"Did the priest say that to your wife?''

"Not like that, no. Some priests are dumb, but not this one. This one's a bright cookie. He knows his onions. He's not gonna say a word about it. He's gonna work it from behind our backs, understand?''

"Yeah. That's what you say.''

"It's clear and simple. I can see it comin'. Nuns, I got nothin' against them either, yuh know...''

"All right, but I don't quite see where I come in to all this.''

"That's just it, Lebeuf, yuh're a fella with an education. Yuh got your B.A., yuh go to university and all that. Maybe yuh could give me a hand.''

"Give you a hand?''

"Yeah. I thought that maybe yuh could give Gisèle sort of a little exam without her knowing...''

Lebeuf ran his hand across his chin. He did not want to be part of all this. "Listen Bill, that's not my bag. As far as studying goes, I can manage. But when it comes to giving a test, I wouldn't know what to ask her. You should ask her teacher.''

"Talk about the teacher! I thought about that, see. But I'm not that dumb! They all stick together, understand.''

"How's that?''

"Teachers and nuns are like peas in a pod. The more pupils they get the more jobs they have, don't yuh see. Bill wasn't born yesterday. I ain't got much education, but I got my eyes open. Watch out.''

54

Lebeuf shook his head. A very French-Canadian streak it was, a universal mistrust, the fear of being rooked.

"That's a bit far-fetched."

"Not a bit. I know what I'm talking about." Bill retracted, afraid of having annoyed his companion. "Maybe yuh're right, Lebeuf. That type of thing's not quite my line. But yuh see, I can't trust a teacher. For another thing, twenty-two bucks a month, that's money. Come fall, Gisèle could take a job in a factory and give us a hand. Between you and me, on my thirty-eight dollars a week, we have a bitch of a time making ends meet — I don't have to tell yuh that."

Lebeuf was moved. He could remember his miserable childhood. His father had been a drunken docker. Never any money at home. At twelve, Jules had been shoveling snow in the winter, working as a delivery boy for the corner grocery store. He had only started his *cours classique* at the age of twenty. Had he been able to pursue his studies more regularly, perhaps, he would have written a few books by now. "Yeah, it's hard. I know. I went through it."

Bill seemed embarrassed. "I don't mean to complain, yuh know, but I just wanna say that... with yuh, Lebeuf, with yuh I'd feel safer about it. Yuh wouldn't be pullin' the wool over my eyes. Yuh could put it to me straight if yuh wanted..."

Bill stopped, cocked an ear. They just had time to turn around; Lévêque stood in front of them. He had blown out his lantern so as not to attract attention.

"Rotten weather, eh boys?" said the foreman, hands behind his back, rocking on his heels.

"Yeah, not nice at all," answered Bill. He paused and then added. 'I had somethin' to discuss with Lebeuf, so we came here to talk about it."

"I don't say nothin'," said Lévêque. "Did I say some-

55

thing?'' He stood there expecting an answer.

''No, yuh didn't say nothin.' '' said Bill.

''Usually your cars are clean. I didn't say nothin' and I won't say nothin' either. Usually you guys don't waste your time. I didn't say nothin'. Once in a while, when the cars are clean, I... You're not like Bouboule...''

''Bouboule is old,'' said Lebeuf. ''He's got rheumatism.''

''I didn't say nothing,'' said Lévêque. ''Did I say anything?''

''No,'' answered Bill, ''yuh didn't say nothing.''

''Still, I'll tell you this much. Get farther inside so the others don't see you. That's all I'm asking. I didn't say nothin.' '' At that point, he pussyfooted out swinging his lantern, still unlit.

Bill and Lebeuf took a few steps between two cars toward the inside of the barns.

''All right,'' said the student, ''I'll see what I can do.''

''Atta boy, Lebeuf! I knew yuh wouldn't let me down. The wife and her funny ideas. Yuh can drop over for a game o' cards 'n yuh can have a little talk with Gisèle.''

''Good.''

''I'll let you know about it, anyway. Yuh might have a little surprise besides.''

They could not chat any longer. Lévêque would be back for sure in five minutes. They headed for their respective cars.

'Well, now we'll have to scrape off that damn tar,'' said Bill.

VIII

"Where's Langevin?" asked Sillery as he walked into the Tigre d'argent. He seemed worried.

Weston shrugged. "I have no idea."

"You were supposed to meet him here?" asked Lebeuf.

"Yes, it's very important. I have things to discuss with him."

Augustin glanced again at the entrance. On the walls, twisted tropical trees with wild animals in their branches were painted in gaudy colors; over the spectators' heads, an enormous tiger, with gaping mouth and outsized claws, was outlined in a pouncing position against a wide, light purple background. Here and there across the hall ceiling, hanging fixtures with yellow bulbs gave off their cones of light.

"Well," said Augustin as he took a seat, "he must have been held up." His voice betrayed disappointment.

"He must be hanging around in some cathouse," said Lebeuf. "That's all he thinks about."

Sillery took a long cigarette holder out of his pocket. "Gentlemen, youth must have its fling. Remember your own misspent ardors."

He suddenly changed the subject as if the matter was not worth further mention. "And which divine liquor, sirs, flows down your eloquent throats tonight?"

"Scotch," said Lebeuf. "Ken just got his check."

"Excellent, gentlemen, wonderful!"

But Augustin was not listening. He had just intercepted a passing waiter. "Three more. Oh, yes, by the way," he lowered his voice "there wouldn't be a message for me at the front desk? Sillery? Augustin Sillery?"

The waiter knew nothing, but he went to find out.

"Is it worrying you?" asked Lebeuf.

"Me? Not in the least!" Augustin lit up a cigarette. He was surprised at the acuteness of his disappointment. That very afternoon, he had been silly enough to phone Langevin, pretending that he wished to borrow a book. A book! And they were supposed to see each other tomorrow at the university. Langevin had been reluctant about the meeting.

"I checked with them; there's no message, sir," announced the returning waiter.

"Thanks very much. It doesn't matter," answered Sillery, slipping a dollar bill into the waiter's hand. "But if someone calls, would you be so kind as to let me know."

"Yes, sir."

Augustin turned towards his partners. They had started talking again.

"I have nothing against philology," Lebeuf was saying. "If somebody wants to specialize in that, it's quite all right. But for us Québécois it's not what we need at all. What we need are massive doses of modern French to compensate for what we hear around here all day long..."

"Allow me to slip in a word of dissent," interrupted Augustin in a shrill voice. The dandy puffed on his cigarette a few times with an air of indifference as if he had finished talking. Lebeuf was about to open his mouth when the same voice, strangely shrill, cut him off. "My opinion, I am sorry to admit, is diametrically opposed to yours. This scotch is foul," he added turning to Weston, "absolutely foul. Doesn't matter anyway. We have long gone past the childish stage of drinking for pleasure." He raised his finger in a scholarly manner. "It has become a question of principle, a sacred principle, one of those principles which..."

"Enough," said Lebeuf.

"Very well, then. To come back to our little academic problem, let me simply remind you that from the linguistic point of view, we have a bad conscience here in French Canada, as our learned friend, Lebeuf here, has so often pointed out."

Augustin paused to appraise the big man's reaction. But Lebeuf remained placid. "Whether one speaks good French or bad French," continued Sillery, "does not change the general principle at all. If one speaks well, one feels different from the rest and suffers as a kind of misfit. On the other hand, gentlemen, should one speak poorly, one's conscience will warn him that he should speak well. In both cases, one finds oneself in a state of existential factitiousness."

"Yeah," said Lebeuf, who was getting ready to retort.

"But listen, gentlemen, listen!" Sillery raised his left hand and glanced furtively at his watch. *Nine-thirty. He won't show up.* "In either case, philology is a valuable aid. In demonstrating the relativity of all languages and their constant evolution, it makes one feel less singular, less of an outcast..."

"Sure, but those are theories, and..."

"I really cannot see why you object, my dear, you less than anyone."

Jules gave him a puzzled glance. Sillery seemed to be loosening up a little.

"Philology offers you an ideal cushion! And 'On the cushion of evil, it is Satan thrice-powerful who rocks for so long ...' "he quoted.

"Just say what you have to say."

"Quite simple, my dear." Augustin raised his glass and wet his lips. "Very simple, I presume — a simple hypothesis, mind you—that you try to express yourself in written French, and that your endeavor does not always meet with success. Therefore..."

"Yeah!"

"Therefore," continued Sillery, raising his forefinger, "nothing more convenient than to blame the scarcity of your masterpieces on the linguistic environment surrounding you. An environment which is governed by the quasi-ineluctable laws of philological and semantic evolution and which..."

"Just a minute," interrupted Lebeuf, "just a minute! That would be too convenient. If people really thought like that, all they'd have to do is sit back and do nothing..."

"I would say," objected Weston, "that it may be lucky for you. You have the chance of belonging to a different milieu which has a slightly different language. That's a distinctiveness right within your reach."

"Yes, yes, but listen," said Jules, his speech becoming more animated. "Different environment is okay. But the milieu you want to write about, you're immersed in it. And if it's disorganized, indifferent and incoherent, you..."

Sillery got up in a rush, scraping his chair on the floor. "Nothing, gentlemen, would warm my heart more than to extend these miry palavers till rosy-fingered dawn, but imperative duties call for my presence elsewhere."

"If we see Langevin," asked Ken, "do you have a message for him?"

A finger on his lips, Sillery feigned surprise. "Langevin? Oh yes, that's right! No, no message at all. I'll see him some other time."

Cigarette holder between thumb and forefinger, he strutted out his usual way. He bemoaned his own lack of will power. He hated himself for being so weak. *I should have stayed and gone on with the discussion as if nothing had happened.*

IX

Out on the sidewalk, a rapid glance to the right and left assured him that Langevin was not in sight. The sky was heavy and overcast. A blurry halo hung around the street lamps. A few prostitutes in gaudy dresses were walking the stretch in front of the cabaret. The cosmopolitan crowd of males who always haunt lower Saint Lawrence Street were eyeing them. Some stopped to haggle. *If only I could want them, it would make things so much easier.* The girls never bothered with him. Occasionally, some would make a perfunctory and half-hearted proposal to him. *They sense it, the sluts.* He gritted his teeth. A nasty urge came over him to pick up one of them, any one, and go up to a room. He had done it a couple of times. But the experiences had disgusted him. No, tonight there was one thing for him to do, only one thing. First walk the red-light district with his eyes open. If he met Langevin, pretend he was surprised. Then, make the rounds of the cabarets. Finally, tire himself out, drink himself into a stupor.

The student was walking toward Saint Elisabeth. The red-brick houses, dimly lit behind the flickering light of lamp posts, displayed rough façades with slotted shutters. As they moved along, some passersby peeped through the mysterious slots from which voices came. *Disgusting.* At the entrance of a dark porch Augustin undid his bow tie and two buttons of his shirt, then lit a big cigar. That would make him look more virile. He walked on, forcing himself to make his gait heavier, like Lebeuf's.

A raspy woman's voice summoned him from inside the house. "Come and see me, good-looking!"

Sillery felt an intense pleasure, but it was short-lived. The thought of Langevin struck him again like a dagger. *Drink, get drunk as a lord.* Why could he not get out of his skin? Escape his own self, for a few moments even? *Drink, drink right away.* But he could see no bar around.

"Holy Jesus! councha look where yuh goin'?"

"Sorry, I wasn't paying attention."

The man walked away, muttering vague threats. Augustin hurried on his way. Langevin was going to pay for this nonsense. He was not going to get away with it. *Where can he be now?* He might have gone to meet Lebeuf and Weston over at the Tigre. Sillery hesitated for a moment. *No. I'm not going back there. I made a fool of myself once, and once is enough.* He noticed a tavern nearby and stumbled in.

"One large Molson."

It was a dive of the worst sort. Dirty, slimy tables. Sodden drinkers wallowing in the stench of sweat. Augustin filled his glass and drank it in one gulp. He hated beer, and this beer was lukewarm, almost hot. *So much the better.* He poured himself another glass. He was beginning to feel vaguely nauseated. *So much the better.* He managed to down a few more gulps. Close to him, an old man, tearful and bleary-eyed, muttered unintelligible words to himself. *He is happier than I am.* Sillery could not stay there any longer. He had to move on, to do something.

"Here," he said, placing the bottle in front of the old man, "it's still half full."

He dashed out and ran up to Craig Street, walked into a café and ordered a glass of wine, which he drank standing at the bar. He walked out again, jacket folded under his arm, sweating. He went to a third tavern, where he had two shots of straight whiskey... He was beginning to feel better. The floor was swaying under his feet. *It's a matter of method and determination; it doesn't take evil genius.* Close to him, their elbows on the table, two men were playing heads or tails. They were tossing their quarters clumsily up into the smoke-filled air and observing the outcome with furrowed brows. They did not seem to be deriving any pleasure out of the game. Augustin walked up to their table.

"Can three play?" he asked.

One of the men moved his chair to make room. "Jump in, friend. The loser pays the round."

All three coins were flipped at once. Augustin lost twice and then won.

One of the fellows hailed a waiter. "The same thing, three times."

He was gummy-eyed, and his voice was hoarse. He gulped his three shots one after the other while the second man mixed his into his beer. A girl came prowling around the table.

"If you've got money to lose, okay," said the chap with the hoarse voice. "Otherwise, so long."

The girl shrugged and went away. The game resumed. Augustin won, lost, then won once more. Five glasses were now lined up before him. *What a stupid game.* He swallowed three, throwing back his head. It seemed to him that the ceiling was coursing like a river. He got on his feet.

"See you around," he said.

He went out. The air was cold and damp, but Sillery could not feel its nip. *That's it! I'm drunk!* He stared dumbly at the breath that billowed from his mouth like cigarette smoke. He threw his jacket over his shoulder and walked to Saint Antoine. A few Negroes walked by without paying any attention to him. Strains of jazz, muffled by the purring of a fan, could be heard coming from the inside of a café. Augustin decided to go in. On a stage at the back, a vaudeville act was being performed. A colored female singer in a fire-red dress was writhing like a snake and screeching a spiritual as two great lumps of men in sailor suits punctuated the song with wild yells. Not one table was free. *What am I doing here?* Augustin headed for the men's room. His head was spinning. *I must look like a sot.* An old Negro with a shiny skull received him smilingly and proceeded to dab his forehead with a cool towel. "There, gov'nor!" He spoke in English with a heavy southern drawl. "There's nuttin' li' a coool towel to put a maan ba' on 'is feet, yessuh!"

Augustin carefully washed his face with cold water. The Negro helped him button his shirt and fix his bow tie. The student felt reinvigorated. The attack was over. He had a look at his watch. *Eleven-thirty! Time really goes by fast.* Lebeuf and Weston were undoudtedly still at the Tigre. Sillery now felt fit to meet them. Their company was worth more than solitude. And what if Langevin was with them? *We'll see.* Augustin slipped a tip into the Negro's hand and walked away.

X

A few minutes later, Augustin reappeared at the Tigre. He had been right; his two friends were still talking at the same table. But there was no trace of Langevin. Sillery felt a slight twinge in the pit of his stomach. *Doesn't matter. I'll get even with him some other time.* His aim now was to make up for what he had done earlier in the evening. He strutted over to his cronies' table.

Lebeuf greeted him with a grunt.

"Did you find Langevin?" asked Weston.

'Langevin? No. You're looking for him?"

Ken stared at him.

"Oh, Langevin! Yes. Yes, I remember now." *The bastards! They must've talked about it after I left.* "No, I haven't seen him." Augustin took out his cigarette holder and was soon blowing smoke rings.

"Cathouses open?" asked Weston.

"Probably," answered Sillery in his high-pitched voice. "At least I believe they are. But having conscientiously masturbated before leaving the paternal shelter and as a result feeling no compulsion to resort to the good offices of those institutions, I did not go and confirm *de peni,* if you'll allow the Latin phrase, whether the places in question were open or closed."

The American smiled and Lebeuf lifted his eyes from his glass.

"To compensate," continued Sillery, "I made the acquaintance of an adorable creature." The dandy paused for an instant, dramatically pulled his cigarette holder from his mouth and got up on his feet.

He's gonna give us one more of his tirades thought Weston.

"It was in the horror of the dead of night," started Sillery very histrionically. "As I was strolling within the winding recesses of our metropolis, I made my way into a dive on Clark Street wherein for but a paltry quarter one is copiously served moonshine in tumblers smelling of urine and dishwater. Up yours, gentlemen!" He raised his glass in a toast and had a few sips.

"The peculiar thing about that place," he continued, "was that the drinks served there affected one's organism in the most wonderful and unexpected ways. Sometimes, one went blind. Other times, one went deaf. On occasion, one suffered urinary retention, ordinarily followed by acute prostatitis requiring emergency surgery. At other times — alas, such was my case — one must be satisfied with common drunkenness and its wake of vomiting of greater or lesser duration. To you, gentlemen." He clinked glasses with Ken, took a few steps around the table before finally straddling a chair, elbows propped against the back.

Lebeuf was scrutinizing him pensively. *If only he were willing to apply himself to serious things*. Sillery showed better command of language than he did. There was no doubt about that. *Maybe precisely because his words are devoid of meaning*. The big man tossed the question in his mind for a few moments. What was amazing was that Sillery seemed to get caught up in his own stories.

The dandy suddenly jumped back to his feet to dramatize an important event. "Now then, as I was barfing for the sixth time, bent over my spittoon, a 'thick Maelstrom' worthy of Huysmans's pen, I heard in the distance such a shattering burp that I raised my unsober head to see who was throwing up with such Sartrian conviction. It was then I saw her! Judging by her pale green complexion, the sweaty salt and pepper locks streaming down her face, the way her dress was all unbuttoned and stained, the manner in which her fingers trembled violently and umpteen details that would take too long to enumerate, I immediately noticed that she was from an excellent family.''

Weston guffawed as Lebeuf shook his head and rubbed his chin. The dandy was warming up.

''What lofty passion had summoned such a delicate creature to this den of existentialism? That was what, gentlemen, I never even had the time to ask myself. Quelling my own attacks of nausea, heeding only my courage, I dashed toward her, mindless of the frothy groans of prostrate drunks whom I trampled as I rushed on.'' He had put down his glass and was enacting the scene. 'I seized her and took her to an adjoining room, laid her on the bed, relieved her of 'useless frills that hung heavy on her,' and so, sirs, this night I lost my virginity.'' His face had assumed an expression of panic. ''Let this be confidential among ourselves, gentlemen. Don't go and blab about it!''

''Don't worry,'' answered Lebeuf as he consulted his watch.

Sillery's act was over. Jules remembered that, at midnight, he had to meet Margot at the restaurant where she worked. He got up.

''You're goin'?'' asked Weston.

''Yeah. Got to meet the chick.''

The American got up too. He was burning to ask Jules how his relations with Margot were going, but he refrained. ''Well, I'm gonna do a special and go to bed at a decent hour tonight.'' he said.

"Come now, gentlemen; you can't be serious!" said Sillery, a hint of apprehension in his voice. The prospect of staying alone at such an early hour terrified him. He would have to start all over again. "Behold, gentlemen, these Circean cups offering their dizzying lips to you! You cannot turn up your noses at their charms!"

"We'll kiss 'em some other time," quipped Lebeuf. He zipped his coat up and went out with Weston, as Augustin stayed behind sadly, sitting with his elbows on the table.

XI

Since the wind had lifted the fog and the sky was now clear, Lebeuf and Margot decided to walk home. She affectionately tucked her arm under his. She felt good. Jules had come to pick her up. He still loved her then. It required only a little patience on her part. He would certainly end up by marrying her. Margot turned to him. He went on in his customary heavy gait, his hands in his pockets, no expression on his face.

"Jules, y'know who I met at the restaurant the day before last?"

"No idea."

"The Péladeau girl, you know, the one I told you I went to school with her sister in Maisonneuve?"

"Oh?"

Lebeuf had never heard about the person in question. "And guess what?"

Jules shrugged. Her roundabout way of bringing up trivial news annoyed him.

"Y'know what? I never mentioned it to you before 'cause she told me not to say anything. Well, y'know what? She's Bill's wife!"

"Bill? Bill who?"

"Bill who? Bill Lafrenière, who do you think! The guy that works with you on the streetcars. You must know him."

"Oh yeah," answered Lebeuf, sounding a trifle more interested.

70

"And d'y'know what? That's not all. We've been invited to their place for a game of cards on Sunday." Marguerite uttered the last sentence with slight apprehension. Jules never took her out in company. "She told me that you had arranged it with Bill. I just said that if it was okay with you, it was okay with me, being as you'd already arranged it with Bill..."

"Yeah."

Margot went back on the defensive. "What did I do wrong again? I told her it was all right with me, being as..."

"Nothing, nothing, you haven't done anything..."

Why had he gotten involved in that exam business? He ought to have foreseen the complications it would entail. Now it was too late to back down. *Besides, it wouldn't be fair, now that I have a chance to help out a fellow man.* Only it was too bad that Margot had become involved. How could there be a test in the middle of a game of cards? Bill had not thought about it.

"So, we're gonna go? You're gonna come? We're gonna go together Sunday?"

Lebeuf nodded without saying anything.

"I don't know what dress I should wear, though. The brown one is stained down at the hem, and I think it's a bit short. I don't know if I should buy me a new one. What do y'think, Jules? What do you say if I buy a new dress?"

"Wear whatever you like," said Jules in a tired voice.

Margot did not say any more. He would go, that was the main thing. She could not ask him to be pleasant on top of that.

XII

The noisy clinking of dishes, thrown carelessly onto the cart by a waiter, startled Sillery. He opened his eyes and saw the waiter. He was an old man in his sixties, with a stubble and deep wrinkles, who dragged his heels from one table to another.

The Two-Bit was a lunch counter that catered almost exclusively to men. The old, chipped, granite tabletops, the rows of chairs with racks for trays, the coterie of hobos and night owls appealed to Augustin. This was where he sought shelter in the wee hours of the morning when he did not feel like going home.

Often he sat at one of the tables at the back, under a huge fan that purred and muffled all other noises, jotting down notes — self-criticism, psychological and literary comments, resolutions, descriptions of people and places — on index cards that he always carried in the inside pocket of his jacket.

The waiter had walked away. In the distance, the clinking of dishes knocking together could be heard off and on. *If it hadn't been for that idiot. I could've had my rest.* Sillery had a look at the index card he had been filling out before he fell asleep.

RESOLUTIONS TO BE TAKEN
1. Feign the most complete indifference with Langevin.

2. If need be, go with him to a brothel.

3. Stop acting like a clown in front of Weston and Lebeuf.

The text ended there. Augustin shook his head, then tore the card to bits. No way he was going to stick to those. Maybe the brothel; that was easy. But the other two? So, what was the use? But he couldn't get his mind off his problems. They were too new, too painful. He tried to think, clear his mind. *First Weston and Lebeuf. Then I can handle that young boor.* Sillery rubbed his stinging eyes. *I acted like a sissy back at the Tigre.* The American had all but laughed at his disappointment, while Jules had not even paid attention. That was even more humiliating. *He despises me. I'm nothing but a clown to him.* Fortunately it was easy enough to seek revenge on Lebeuf; all one needed to do was to scoff at his literary endeavors. It was not so easy with Weston. *If only I knew something of his private life.* Then his mind turned to Langevin. He was the one responsible for everything. *He's going to pay for this.* But how? Feign indifference? Would that not risk losing him? And by the same token let him see how much power he had? Augustin clenched his fists. He was sweating over his whole body. *What am I going to do? What's going to become of me?* He cast a bewildered look around him, made a motion to get up, then dropped back into his chair. *Anywhere else it will be the same thing.*

His eyes suddenly lit upon a hobo in a tattered jacket who had sat down at a table next to his and was now staring at him. Augustin relaxed for a while. *He's going to ask me for money.*

"Cigarette, sir?" he said in a rather high-pitched voice that startled the vagrant.

"I wouldn't say no, young man," answered the old man as his trembling hand reached for the package.

His bushy moustache hid part of his mouth. Was he a foreigner? An old farmer? Augustin could not have guessed. The voice was so rough that he had not paid any attention to the accent.

"It wasn't always like this, young man, you know, there was a time when..." He stopped a moment to light his cigarette.

"Life has hard times in store for everyone of us," reflected Sillery.

"Hard times? You can say that again, my young friend. 'Hard times' is right! I've had my share of them. I don't know many who've seen as much as me, you can be sure of that."

Definitely he was not a native Québécois. He did not put that *s* sound between his *t*'s and his *i*'s.

"What you see in front of you is nothing more and nothing less than a Frenchman." The man was doubtless aware that there was nothing better to bring out a Québécois' sympathy. "French from France," he added for precision as he puffed out a cloud of smoke. "From Burgundy. Merchant navy; landed in Halifax on October 12, 1923." He continued puffing vigorously.

"Won't you have a coffee?"

"Wouldn't say no, my young friend. Simply to be polite."

'I'll be right back."

The old man slumped in his chair, looking self-satisfied

Sillery took two coffees, two ham sandwiches and two wedges of pie from the bar and put them in front of the hobo. The old man stuffed half his sandwich in his mouth at once.

"So you've had bad times?" asked Augustin.

The vagrant took time to swallow his mouthful. "As I was saying, my friend, I landed in Halifax on October 12, 1923, merchant marine. Our ship was the *Indomptable* of

74

the Islands and Guyana line." He had another quick bite at his sandwich. "I was fed up with the merchant navy. Can you imagine, three years of it! Three years, as true as you're standing in front of me. And the captain, pardon the expression, was nothing but a pig. Oh, he was a good sailor all right, but he was nothing but a pig just the same." The vagrant wolfed down the rest of his sandwich, grabbed hold of his fork and started on the pie.

"I don't mean to complain, my young friend. A dog's life just the same, to be sure. But if you'll pardon the expression, I'd dipped the wick from Zanzibar to the Dutch Indies, passing through Buenos Aires and Santiago, Chile, along the way." He looked at Sillery as if to see if his words had had some effect.

"In others words," said Sillery, "you had a seven-league wick."

The old man guffawed and wheezed. "You're quite a joker, you! I noticed it right away. The minute I saw you walking in, I said to myself, that young fellow likes to joke. 'A seven-league wick,' as sure as you're sitting there. But still, as things go, it was a dog's life." The hobo forked in another piece of his pie. "So then I said to myself, so much for the merchant navy, away with it and on to Canada. Canada is a young country with a future. As we say, off to Canada. And I had to get out of Halifax fast because, let me tell you, the captain didn't take deserters kindly. So I signed on as a lumberjack up north."

Augustin was lending a distracted ear. Always the same story. Hard times! Nobody wanted to face up to reality.

"...as sure as you're born, it's a matter of letting things work themselves out, you see. Wood galore, my young friend. Chopping, day in, day out. Working something fierce. But you get used to it. At the end of two weeks I could chop down two and a half cords a day, as sure as you're alive." The vagrant paused as he brought his fork to his mouth. "Then all of a sudden, it happened just like that. No warning, nothing, as sure as you sit there."

He had a sip of his coffee and peeked over his cup to see if he had aroused the young man's curiosity. Sillery was staring at the wall blankly. At the other end of the hall, the waiter was still knocking dishes together and dragging his feet. Sleepers stirred in their chairs, opening their eyes briefly and then falling back to sleep.

"Yeah, that was quite a hard knock, that knock, my young friend."

"A hard knock?"

"As sure as you're there! On the sixth day exactly, on November 26, 1923, one-thirty in the afternoon, a tree fell down on my leg and smashed it in three places. For a knock, that was quite a hard one."

"Yes indeed," said Sillery as he got up. "That was quite a blow. Sorry sir, but I must tear myself away from your captivating conversation."

The hobo touched his battered hat with two fingers; he seemed vexed. "As you wish, my young friend."

Augustin stroke toward the exit. *They're all the same. They refuse to admit that they are responsible.* As soon as he was outside, he took a deep breath. Eastward, in the distance, above the roofs, dawn was spreading its diffused light across the grayish sky. A shiver went through his whole body. He had not even touched his sandwhich. *Twenty-three hours without eating!* Yet he was not hungry. He did not even feel weak. How odd that four years prior the doctor had recommended that Sillery, who was then just out of the sanatorium, lead a "quiet, sheltered life devoid of any violent emotions." Sillery swept his hand across his forehead. A streetcar rattled by. A few workingmen, their lunch pails under their arms, walked by looking gloomy. *I can't go home now!* See his mother's sad eyes, hear his father's ravings? No, he did not feel up to it. He had to tire himself out first, walk a lot or something till he was completely exhausted. Then he would be able to go home and climb into bed.

"Well, for heaven's sake, Sillery! What are you doing around here?"

Augustin was startled. He turned his head, holding back a wince. Bélan, a dunce who had failed his exams in the Literature Department at the end of his first semester, stood next to him.

"Oh, it's you!" said Sillery in his high-pitched voice. "How are you, my dear." Bélan reminded him of his father — the same strong bull's neck, porcine eyes, ruddy face and square shoulders. *A boor*. Augustin had always avoided him.

"What in the devil are you doing here at six in the morning? You look half dead!" said Bélan.

Augustin regained his composure. "As you can see, my dear, I'm sniffing in the morning breeze. I am savoring the lush smells of Montreal's belly. 'Time when the swarming mischievous dreams have the tawny adolescents toss in their beds...' Thanks to your too brief stay among us, you have no doubt preserved the memory of those sweet lines."

Any allusion to his failure annoyed Bélan. *Goddamn fruit* he said to himself. "By the way I was looking for you," he remarked. "I spent part of the night with Langevin."

Sillery repressed a shudder. *Be careful*. He bit his lips.

"I thought I understood he was to meet you at the Tigre?" said Bélan.

Augustin pulled his cigarettes out of his pocket. "You smoke?" Bélan had one. Sillery lit his and said with indifference. "Langevin? Yes, well, I had to meet Weston and Lebeuf. He had led me to believe that he might be there, but we left much earlier than usual..." Augustin held two fingers out to the former student. "Well, my dear, it was an unspeakable pleasure to meet you again."

Bélan did not move. "I haven't told you everything. We went to the whorehouse together."

Sillery stopped smoking. His nostrils started to quiver. "Oh really? Very interesting! Tell me more. You've got time for a coffee?"

"I was going to suggest that, but you seemed in a hurry."

Augustin threw both arms up affecting surprise. "Me? Not in the least. Besides, we see so little of each other. After you, if you please."

They walked into a restaurant.

XIII

Saint Catherine Street was getting crowded. The big stores had not yet opened, but late-coming staff were hurrying in. Arriving at Phillips Square, Sillery stopped. *One of the city's highlights. Crummy if you ask me.* Street life, which usually brought some form of distraction, had no effect on him now. His earlier conversation with Bélan was still painfully ringing in his ears. Langevin had gone to the brothel with that brute! He had made love with a whore! While he was waiting for him at the Tigre. *The dirty scum!* Why had he done that? Why? Why at least had he not gone with Sillery? *I was ready to go with him, I'd even jotted that down on my index card at the Two-Bit.* Sillery had never felt such a searing pain. *It can't go on like this.* Who was the cause of his torture? A little runt of a pretentious brute who was trying to play tough. A vulgar skirt-chaser. Not that even, a whoremonger. *Why do I hang on to him like that?* There were hundreds of thousands of young men in Montreal, far more interesting, certainly less conceited... Augustin felt his legs go soft under him. *It's because I haven't eaten.* He took a few more steps and dropped on a nearby stone bench, across from the entrance to the public restrooms. Facing him on the other side of the street was a huge billboard: HOWARD'S — BUY BRITISH. There was a time when such an advertisement would have affronted him; today it left him indifferent. *Why not? After all, those people are businessmen. No doubt that's a way for them to up their profits.* He immediately dismissed the problem.

He rubbed his eyes with the back of his hand, which was hot and clammy. *Won't there ever be an end to all this?* He was not thinking about Langevin. Langevin was a mere consequence. He was thinking about his own predicament: himself, his being, his life. *Why me and not others?* He would try to resign himself. *Nothing to do about it. Like being born one-eyed and one-armed.* Nothing to do about it? Not so sure. This was a philosophical peculiarity, rather than a physical one... The eternal question of free will. *Insoluble like all the important questions.* Augustin recalled *War and Peace* and Tolstoi's debate: feeling of freedom within one's conscience; rigid unfolding of causes and effects in the external world. *Insoluble but corrosive.*

"This yer paper?"

"Beg your pardon?"

The old man was pointing at a newspaper lying on the bench. "The paper," he repeated.

"No, no, go ahead and take it."

Augustin got up. He did not feel up to another conversation with a hobo. Perfunctorily he started to trudge eastward. His heart was beating hard; he felt vaguely sick to his stomach. *I must have something to eat.* The sidewalk was like a long conveyor belt full of its usual load of shoppers and businessmen. Streetcars, packed like sardines, moved along in spurts, cruising taxis jammed the flow of traffic, annoyed motorists angrily released their frustrations on their horns. *All these people are happy; they have something to do, to look forward to, a goal.* To his right, a chef, his hat puffed like a balloon, was tossing a pancake up from his pan. Sillery walked in and sat in a booth on a bench. *If only I could hold something in my stomach.* He had a look at his watch. *Classes start in an hour*. But he was not going to go to the university today. He would not risk meeting Langevin in the state he was in. The waitress came over. Augustin ordered a bacon omelet, which he just nibbled at. The food was insipid and stodgy. *As long as it stays down all right*. He made himself swallow a mouthful of coffee. *As soon as I'm finished, I'll go home*. His father was already on his way to the office. Augustin would be able to slip unseen into his room. *With a few hours of sleep, I'll be able to face the situation more calmly*.

XIV

Preparations for the card party at Bill's place were in full swing. Since the sweeper had just received his pay check, they had decided to do things in style. Mrs. Lafrenière had bought a large ham, hors d'oeuvres and peanuts, and she had just taken a big, sweet-smelling angelfood cake out of the oven.

Bill had not wasted his time either. After taking his four brats to his brother's place in Rosemount so they would not get underfoot, he had gotten two dozen Dows, a bottle of Vermouth and forty-ounces of whiskey, which now sat in the old icebox next to the ham. In spite of everything, the sweeper felt uneasy. He kept pacing back and forth between the kitchen and the living room, interfering with his wife's work. No matter how often she pleaded with him to calm down or go for a walk, he kept it up. He wanted to make sure that everything would be first class. Looking worried, his jaws chewing away as if on some everlasting candy, he was sometimes gripped by fits of childish enthusiasm.

"We're gonna have ourselves one helluva nice li'l party, eh, mother."

"Yeah, well I hope you're gonna behave yourself, Bill. Not too heavy on the booze, eh? An' no swearin' either," warned Mrs. Lafrenière, a small, dried-up woman in her forties with a wan, already wrinkled face.

She was worried about Lebeuf's visit. Bill had mentioned the student, his education and his courageous attitude in the face of the Company's injustices so often that Mrs. Lafrenière had come to picture him as some kind of superman.

The tiny woman was having a last look at her setting of the kitchen table when she cried out in panic.

"Good God, whatsa matter, Estelle?" asked Bill.

"Can you imagine, I was about to forget the ice cream! Gisèle, Gisèle," she intoned in her shrill voice. "I don't know what it is she's doing. She's been locked up in her room for almost an hour instead of giving me a hand. Gisèle!"

Bill was not interested in the matter. Bottles were lined up in the upper part of the icebox. The ham was well done. The rest was of little importance. Dessert was not his concern. He never ate sweets. That was women's and kids' stuff.

Gisèle finally showed up in a pink taffeta dress trimmed with pale green flowers. Her black, slightly impish eyes, shone with an unusual gleam today. Bill gazed at her with satisfaction.

"Run over to Missus Turgeon and get three quarts of ice cream, an' come back right away, you hear?" said Mrs. Lafrenière.

Gisèle took the money Bill handed her and bounded out with the quick agility of an adolescent.

She was no less excited than her parents by the prospect of the visit. For several days, she had felt that there was something in the air, something that had to do with her. One night, when she was in her room studying, she had overheard Bill and Mrs. Lafrenière talking things over in low voices in the kitchen. By opening the door, Gisèle had been able to snatch bits of their conversation, incomplete, but enough for her to grasp the motive behind Lebeuf's visit. The following night the teenaged girl had slept very little. All of a sudden, her future was being thrown into the hands of that stranger, some enigmatic character who was a sweeper, yet, at the same time, a student. For months, Bill had been raving about Lebeuf. "A tough-minded fella, who's not afraid of anything, and who doesn't do no fancy talkin', a fella that parish priests and white collars have nothing on in no way." As a rule Gisèle did not pay any attention to stories about the Company and workers' unrest. Had these stories come from anyone but her father she would have met them with complete apathy. She had other concerns, concerns of a higher nature. She wanted to pursue her studies past grade nine. She wanted to get out of this miserable place where people talked about nothing except bills to pay, the next pay check and soaring prices. Two of her schoolmates were going on to boarding school next year. She had decided that she, too, would enroll at any cost. The prospect of ending up in a canning factory, like some of her less fortunate girlfriends, made her shiver. Some while back, during the summer holidays, Mrs. Lafrenière had sent her with a message to an aunt at the Maisonneuve Canning Company. The racket of the machines, the lights turned on in the middle of the day amid the stench of oil and sweat, the rows of female workers riveted to their stools like prisoners had left her with a hellish memory. No, she would never agree to work there. She knew about other things, she did. She had read the novels of Delly and of Henri Ardel, borrowed from the school library. She knew that it was possible for a young girl such as herself to meet a rich, handsome young man, bold and refined, and to make him fall deeply in love. She knew that she was pretty. Men's heads turned whenever she walked past them on the street, and they made loose remarks. But those men were nothing but oafs. Noble and pure young men, capable of an everlasting love — where were they? All the interesting novels she had read were set in France. Yet similar heroes must exist in Canada in a big city like Montreal? Was Lebeuf one? What kind of man was he? How should she act with him? A student-sweeper! What could be more inconceivable? And yet, she *had* to adopt some attitude. It was of the utmost importance. Her future and her happiness, it seemed, depended on the impression she would make on this enigmatic stranger.

The young girl shook her head and noticed that she had arrived at Mrs. Turgeon's grocery store. She opened the door.

"Well, here now! Here's the li'l Lafrenière girl!" said the fat shopkeeper. Gisèle could not stand the obese gossip. She was constantly out of breath and stank of sweat, and she talked down to her as if she were a little girl, calling her "dearie."

"I would like three bricks of ice cream, please."

"Three bricks! Looks like the Lafrenières are going all out! Looks like you're gonna eat ice cream!" The fat shopkeeper, wheezing heavily, hobbled over to the freezer. Then she stopped suddenly. "Three bricks? That'll be cash this time, won't it?" Mrs. Turgeon was quite willing to sell staple foods on credit — raising the prices naturally, to cover her risk — but three quarts of ice cream was a bit too much. "Will that be cash or won't it be cash?"

Gisèle felt like smacking her across the face. There were other customers in the store, two men in their shirt sleeves playing the slot machine and drinking Coca Cola.

"I never show up here without any money," snapped the teenager.

"Maybe not you, dearie, maybe not. But some in your family show up a li'l too often. Tell your father I want to have a word with him. Yesterday was his pay day, right?"

Gisèle gritted her teeth. Once Bill had sent her to Mrs.

Turgeon's to get cigarettes on credit. The shopkeeper had refused to let her have any. Since then, she refused to go back to the grocery store without money.

'Here, you can have them then, dearie,'' said the woman as she placed the ice cream on the counter.

"And my name's not dearie, it's Gisèle, Mrs. Turgeon.''

The fat woman, astounded and wide-eyed, put her hands on her hips. "You hear that, you guys?'' she called to the coke-drinking customers. "Her name is Gisèle.''

Both men raised their heads without understanding.

"You heard that? Missy, here, you've gotta treat her with kid gloves these days. Listen, dearie, no kid gloves for you. All your father's talk about sending you to boarding school has gone to your head. Me, when I was your age, maybe my name wasn't Gisèle, but I was working, I was earning my keep.'' She put the bricks of ice cream in a bag and let them drop on the counter. "A dollar twenty.''

Gisèle dropped the money on the counter and went out.

No, it could not go on like this. One way or another, she would escape this place. Her parents did not know anything else. Bill had left school after grade four, and Mrs. Lafrenière had lived in the country until she was fifteen. But Gisèle, at least, knew everybody did not live this way. There were some teenaged girls who did not have to buy on credit, to patch the same old dress four or five times, to swallow the insults of people like Mrs. Turgeon. Fortunately, the dress Gisèle had on today was almost new; in fact she had only worn it three times. Today was when the die would be cast, by a stranger called Lebeuf. Gisèle pursed her lips resolutely. She absolutely had to make a good impression on him.

XV

When she got home, she heard unknown voices coming through the door. Could they be here already? Gisèle had wanted so much to be there when he arrived. Thanks to the hubbub of introductions, she could have observed him unseen. But it was too late now. The evening was off to a bad start. What was more, Gisèle had not had the time to put on her lipstick. Would it be better to sneak through the back lane? No. That would be no use. Her cosmetics were in her bedroom, and Bill would still ask her why she had made a detour. The young girl patted her head to make sure that her hairdo was all right and bit her lips to make them redder. *After all, what does it matter? That's not what he's coming here for.*

She opened the door quickly. Sitting in front of her, slouched in an armchair with his legs crossed, was a kind of giant with a brush-cut and a jacket that seemed too tight at the waist. *It's impossible. That can't be him.* On the right, in a rocker, sat a plump woman, with scarlet lips, who was conversing with her mother.

"Well, here's my daughter," said Bill. "She's been over to the grocery to get ice cream. This is my girl, Lebeuf, my daughter, Gisèle, that I told yuh about. Gisèle, this is Mr. Lebeuf."

Jules got up, looking rather encumbered by his limbs, and held out his hand to the teenager. "It's a pleasure."

Gisèle executed a semblance of a curtsy. Lebeuf's hand

was tough and calloused like her father's. 'How do you do,'' she mumbled, blushing.

A real beauty thought Lebeuf. *I wasn't expecting so much.* Immediately his mind turned to a sketch of Natasha he had seen recently in an illustrated edition of *War and Peace.* Same black hair, thick and wavy; same small face and slim figure; same delicate curve of the breasts that slightly uplifted the bodice of her dress; same deep-set, lively and slightly impish eyes... *How could I have expected that much with such a father!*

"And that's Marguerite over here, Mr. Lebeuf's girl friend," said Mrs. Lafrenière.

Gisèle curtsied in a way reminiscent of the ladies of the old French regime.

"My Lord, don't tell me that's yer daughter! Growin' like a weed. And she is mighty good looking too!"

Gisèle blushed as she idly played with the ice cream, swinging it at arm's length. "Excuse me," she said. "I'll go and put this in the icebox."

She almost ran toward the kitchen. Bill sidled over to Lebeuf like a conspirator. "Well, Lebeuf, whattya think of her?"

Jules nodded his head. "She's a good-looking girl."

The father beamed. "It's not just'cause she's my girl, but she doesn't look bad at all. Whattya think?" he continued as he elbowed his friend.

'She's a real good-looking girl."

Bill rubbed his hands. "Well now then, how about a game of cards?"

"We're all set," said Mrs. Lafrenière.

"What about you, Lebeuf?"

'All right with me," said Lebeuf.

He sat in front of Mrs. Lafrenière, while Bill and Margot played as partners.

"I invited Bouboule too, yuh know," whispered Bill in

88

Jules' ear. "But I told him to come for ten o'clock. When he gets here, yuh can let him have yer place and that'll give yuh a chance to have a chat with Gisèle."

While the cards were being dealt, Gisèle reappeared. She had lipstick on now and had fixed her hair. Lebeuf found her less pretty that way. It took away some of her innocence and spontaneity.

'Gisèle, how about filling Mr. Lebeuf's glass," said Bill. "Lebeuf, you must be thirsty there."

Lebeuf handed his glass over. "Wouldn't say no."

Gisèle noticed once more his huge, hairy, calloused hands. A student? She saw in him nothing different from what she saw in her father's other workmates.

"You think we're gonna have a strike after all?" asked Bill, who wanted to show what kind of a fellow their guest was.

"Maybe in the fall," said Lebeuf.

"The company's bigshots pretend they're not makin' any profits. What do you think of that?"

Jules made a vague gesture. This did not seem to him to be the right time to open up such a discussion.

"Whattya think?" repeated Bill.

Gisèle came back with the glass of whiskey. She must have overheard the question. She stood there with her eyes fixed on Lebeuf, looking interested. He made up his mind to answer.

"I'll tell you what I think. Before the war, in '39, one company share was worth, let's say, a hundred dollars. Since then, they've gone up to something like two hundred and seventy-five dollars. And bear in mind that raise isn't taxable. Capital gains, they call that. Today they're complaining that they're not making even six percent profit. But if you figure out their real expenditures, they're making in the vicinity of thirteen, fourteen or fifteen percent."

"Well, of course!" agreed Bill, who understood nothing of these calculations.

He gave his wife a look that meant *your parish priest doesn't know all that*.

"Despite the profits piling up," continued Lebeuf, "try and find one, only one of those big shareholders who'll donate anything worth mentioning to our libraries or our universities? No use mentioning museums. It's a shame."

Bill rubbed his chin. "Well yeah, what can yuh say. But they'd be better to give us a bit more in wages."

Lebeuf agreed with a gesture. "I'm for decent wages a hundred percent. But that's a different thing. It doesn't last. You spend your wages, whereas education remains, it's solid."

Mrs. Lafrenière pinched her lips. She was not against education either, far from that, but you had to keep your head well screwed on your shoulders. You could take off with high-faluting theories as long as you were not married. But for a mother and housewife with five children, it was a different kettle of fish.

"My lord, him and his speeches. He's always makin' speeches," said Marguerite. "Are we playin' cards or not?"

Mrs Lafrenière cleared her throat. "Well, Bill, we might as well get started."

"Yeah, let's get down to it," answered Bill.

The discussion had not turned out the way he had wanted. Estelle must not have caught on. But he put these thoughts out of his mind. The evening had to be a complete success. "Yeah, well are we gonna play for two bits a game or what?"

"That's okay with me," said Lebeuf.

Gisèle sat between her mother and Marguerite. Cards bored her, but she did not want to miss any of Lebeuf's

90

comments. Her father was right in saying that this sweeper was different from the rest. *He'll undestand me.* Too bad he had the manners of a farmer and went out with a simpleton like Margot...

"Trump and retrump! By God, we've gotcha!" Lafrenière had gotten up and was banging the table with his fist.

"Bill!" warned his wife, casting a worried look in the direction of Marguerite. Bill was rubbing his hands with satisfaction.

"You play hard," said Lebeuf.

The sweeper sat down and swallowed all his whiskey in one gulp. "We weren't born yesterday, were we, Miss Marguerite?"

"No, that's for sure."

Bill was attracted by Margot. She gave him a lift. *Big enough, but not too big, white skin, firm breasts and easy-going too...* He compared her to his wife, skinny and flat since her last miscarriage. *Lebeuf must never get bored.*

New hands were dealt. His brow furrowed, his chin protruding like an old shoe more than usual, Bill pondered his play intensely.

Suddenly the door opened. All raised their heads. Standing in the doorway was Bouboule, shaved and wearing a tie and a thick, brand-new, woolen sweater; he was staring at the group with obvious self-conciousness, his Adam's apple wiggling.

"Bouboule, son of a gun! Come on in. Here's a chair. Sit down. We were just givin' it to them somethin' fierce."

The old man walked in with some hesitation, shook hands with Lebeuf and Bill and sat apart from the group after he had clumsily greeted the ladies. "Mind if I smoke, Bill?" he asked as he half drew his pipe out of his pocket and made a nodding movement in the direction of the three women.

"Go ahead, Bouboule, go ahead. One more smell isn't gonna make any difference."

Mrs. Lafrenière pinched her lips together once more, but refrained from comment. Besides, Bill was engrossed in the game. Twisting his tongue between his toothless gums, he assumed the posture of a general supervising the movements of his troops. Then suddenly, the trumps and retrumps would ring out and the traditional fist would bang on the table. Or, if he had received a bad hand, he would drop his cards, eyebrows raised with an air of indifference as if the game did not matter at all. In the end he lost the game.

To hide his annoyance, and also to give the visitors a demonstration of what Bouboule was like, he asked him, "Listen there, Bouboule, the word is that we're gonna strike in the fall. Are you with us or against us? I hear that you think we're too well paid."

Bouboule's eyes took on a sudden spark of life, and his Adam's apple momentarily interrupted its endless trek. He responded in his soft voice, "The goddamn sons..." He cast a hostile look at the women. There was no way to express one's opinions in the presence of the weaker sex. "I'm ready to last three years," he continued. "The sons of... Even if I have to eat rabid cows and scrounge around garbage cans."

"Some say they're gonna take the pensions away from those who strike," said Bill, casting a knowing look towards the others.

Bouboule nearly dropped his pipe from his mouth. He had only three years to go before drawing his pension. He was sure that the company was contemplating such an infamous deed. He momentarily forgot where he was. "The goddamn slimy sons of bitches! I warned you, Bill,

92

and I warned the boys over and over again. They don' wanna believe me. I told you they're gettin' ready to shit on us again. They all need their heads shoved down a hole in a outhouse.''

Bill was killing himself laughing, but he felt it unfit to push things any farther because of Marguerite. After all one had to respect good manners. The show had been a success.

"Yeah," he said when he had stopped laughing and reminded himself of the aim of the evening, "yeah, well Lebeuf, wouldn't you like to let Bouboule take your place? In the meantime, Gisèle, it might be a good idea for you to show Mr. Lebeuf your homework books.''

Gisèle blushed and cast a questioning look a Jules. Despite his remarks in favor of education she could not conceive how he would be interested in a schoolgirl's scribblings.

"Show him in your room. You'll be quieter there," suggested Bill.

Lebeuf got up. He might as well get the task over with right away, and being alone with Gisèle would make it easier.

"This way," said Gisèle.

XVI

Her room was small and poorly furnished. The paint on
the iron bed was peeling; an oval mirror was mounted over
a badly varnished table. On the wall hung a plaster
crucifix and a picture of Gisèle in her First Communion
dress. A beat-up dresser, a very old mahogany chair and
an unmatched one that doubtless came from the kitchen
completed the furnishings.

Gisèle gestured to Jules to sit down. She took a seat
facing him, motionless, her hands resting on her knees.
The silence deepened.

"You want to see my exercise books?" she asked.

Lebeuf gestured vaguely. "All right, I could have a
look at your composition book."

He began to leaf through the notebook she handed him.
There was a narrative on back-to-school day, another one
on springtime, another on a picnic, then one on a visit to
church. The red-penciled grades ranged between 58 and
72.

"You don't like composition too much, do you?"

Gisèle shook her head. "But I like algebra. I almost
always get 100 in algebra..." She blushed. Such an incli-
nation must have seemed strange for a girl.

"What about geometry? Do you like that too?"

'Yes, but we don't have any this year."

Jules shook his head. "I was never good at figures."

Gisèle looked down. Figures were not important at all,

they were merely a minor subject.

"Let's have a look at your algebra," he said.

There were second and third-degree equations written down clearly and without any erasures. No doubt she had talent for mathematics.

"Yeah, well it looks like you're pretty good with figures. Unfortunately, I'm in a bad position to say anything about that. It's not my specialty, you see."

Gisèle nervously scraped the floor with the tip of her shoe. What did he mean by not his specialty? Any university student must know a whole lot more than she did in all fields. For sure he was just avoiding commitment.

"Do you know why I'm here?" asked Lebeuf all of a sudden.

"I... I think, to give me a test."

Lebeuf agreed, then hesitated for a few seconds. "You know the test wasn't my idea. Bill's the one who..."

He stopped talking. Gisèle, eyes lowered, hands clamped together was staring at the floor.

"Why do you want to go on studying?"

Gisèle had been expecting that question. She had even prepared a long, eloquent answer. But now she felt panicked when faced with Lebeuf. Would he not laugh at her, think her uppity if she touched on culture, good manners?

She bit her lips and put it very simply. "My parents want me to go and work at the factory next year." She regretted her answer at once. "Not only that. Mom and Dad, they..."

Gisèle resumed tracing circles on the floor with her foot. She suddenly felt utterly discouraged. Why had she mentioned the factory? Lebeuf would think that she was lazy and unconcerned with the fate of her parents. She had a lump in her throat.

Jules gazed at her pensively: her slender hands, her thin

neck, so thin that the veins protruded, her dark eyes immensely sad now. "Well, obviously," he uttered, as if to himself, "A factory isn't the most interesting of places, especially when you have other plans in mind..."

He could remember the first weeks of his stay in Boston. Standing for eight hours before his power loom, the deafening noise of shuttles, the smell of the wool... He would come back to his room at night numb with fatigue, unable even to read. Often he would flop into bed still dressed and fall into a deep sleep. Yet he had been physically strong; he had been able to hang on; he had recovered soon enough... whereas Gisèle was only a child. He noticed her frail arms, their milky-white skin with delicate bluish veins.

"The factory isn't very interesting," he reiterated. "No doubt about that." No, she was not meant for that type of work. What would become of her after but a few years of such drudgery? She would lose her beauty, her zest, her ambitions...

"What about you? Have you ever worked in a factory?"

"Yes, for three years in Boston." He shook his head as if to drive away some obsessive thought. "You spend a lot of time over an algebra problem?"

"No. I always find them easy. Fifteen, twenty minutes."

"And do you do some on your own sometimes, just for fun?"

Gisèle blushed and hesitated a while. "Yes, sometimes."

She had never mentioned this to anyone. She would have been ridiculed by her schoolmates. Neither did she receive encouragement from her algebra teacher, a grouchy old maid who stuck to the textbook.

Lebeuf shook his head. Obviously, that proved nothing, or almost nothing. At best it was a mere indication. How could he make sure? He ran his hand through his hair. Thousands of talents were being lost in this way year after year for lack of counseling or education. *This is why we turn out so few intellectuals.*

"Next year we would be starting on trig and logs. That's what the teacher..." Gisèle stopped there. Her line sounded too much like a plea, and Lebeuf did not seem to be paying attention.

"Yeah."

Raised voices from what appeared to be a heated argument were heard coming from the dining room. Bill's choppy speech resounded above the others. But even the voice of the protesting Bouboule could be heard.

With a perfunctory gesture, Lebeuf took his pipe out of his pocket and started to blow into it. Then he remembered where he was and put it back in its place. His look wandered across the room. A few brown-jacketed books lay on top of a chest of drawers, next to a hair brush and a comb.

"You read much?" he asked.

Gisèle hesitated. "Not too much. A book once in a while, whenever I get a chance."

She glanced quickly at Lebeuf. She read a great deal, of course, sometimes two books a week. Novels most of the time, never any serious works. The school librarian, a half-senile old nun, had often chided her about that. So now Gisèle simply abstained from library books. Or if she did borrow one, she asked for "serious books" — spiritual exercises, the psychology of adolescents, lives of saints — and a novel. Only she never read the serious books.

"Yeah," commented Lebeuf.

He opened his mouth to add something, but the loud voices from the dining room had reached a higher pitch.

97

Everybody was talking at once. Jules got up. "Well, I guess we've said all we have to say. I'll go back to the card players before they start jumping at each other's throats."

Gisèle got up too. There was a look of panic in her eyes, and she grabbed Lebeuf's arm. "What are you going to do?" The voice was almost pleading.

Jules looked at her for a moment, then replied, "Don't know yet. I'll speak to Bill tomorrow. We'll try to do something."

Gisèle tightened her grip, lowered her head and whispered quickly, but with a note of determination. "In any case, if I can't study next year, I'm gonna run away from home, and I'll never set foot in this house again. Understand? Never again. You can tell that to Papa, tomorrow."

She left the room almost running. Lebeuf did not see her again that evening.

XVII

Lebeuf slowly closed his book and put his elbows on the folding table that served him for a desk. This morning, having decided to work, he had gotten up at the same time Margot left for the restaurant. He had just been reading a chapter of *6 octobre, Présentation de Paris à cinq heures du soir,* and now he was ready. He uncapped his ballpoint pen, opened a cardboard-covered copybook and began to write immediately. The sentences came to him easily. He had often turned them over in his mind. He wrote:

Strongly arched toward the middle by an ancient volcano, the island split the gigantic river like the stem of a vessel. It was night. The city lay sleeping. Leaning on his elbows against the parapet of the observatory, his back turned on the Mount Royal chalet, Jérôme was contemplating the huge metropolis.

A few hundred feet down, streaks of light, serried and regular as hemming stitches, flowed along the beds of the main arteries. Farther down, two other rosaries of light straddled the river, revealing the location of the Victoria and Jacques Cartier bridges where the headlights of a few cars could be seen moving slowly. Strewn all over town, other lights formed dispersed constellations. But most buildings were dark, their presence revealed only through mottled shadows.

Jérôme had been contemplating the swarming for hours. It was more fascinating for him than the movement of stars above. He was well acquainted with this scene. Each curve in the layout represented a well-known place visited a hundred times and to be visited again in days to come. Sighing, he stretched his long, thin arms and decided to walk home.

Lebeuf paused to reread his text. He had always dreamt of a "grand" opening. First a panorama, an overlook. Then he would introduce the characters, set the conflict and knit the plot. But as he read, his face grew somber. This wasn't it at all! Much too bombastic. A panorama was all right, but to what did it correspond? Where was the human element, the warmth, the throbbing of life? *This was schoolboy stuff.* To begin with, what was "strongly arched" there for, and "ancient volcano," and that "stem of a vessel!" Pure imagination! The mountain's "arch," well, that could always stay since Jérôme was standing on top of the mountain. But "ancient volcano" and especially that "stem of a vessel" just did not work at all. How could the hero see the tip of the island, especially at night? One could not mix imaginary elements with visual ones.

After pondering for a few seconds, Jules crossed out the first sentence completely. Then he reread the rest.

It was night. The city lay sleeping. Leaning on his elbows against the parapet of the observatory, his back turned on the Mount Royal chalet, Jérôme was contemplating the huge metropolis.

A few hundred feet down, streaks of light, serried and regular as hemming stitches, flowed along the lines of the main arteries. Farther down, two other rosaries of light straddled the river...

Lebeuf knitted his brow. It was visual, there was no doubt about that. But was it of any interest? No, none. Some guy on a mountain at night. Dreaming. He sees lights. The big man muttered his disgust. *Romanticism of the most trite kind!* That's exactly what it was! *'Cause I speak poorly in reality, I feel obliged to use grand terms when I pick up a pen.* "Mottled shadows," "rosaries of light," "dispersed constellations!" *Shit!* Lebeuf angrily ripped out the pages and flung them into the wastebasket. *Where did I get the idea of starting with a panoramic view?* Quite the contrary, one had to get right down to the subject in the middle of action, adding a few descriptive elements here and there, so as to let the reader develop his own background setting, not impose it on him. *A panoramic setting! Such naiveté! Then why not a full-fledged census of Montreal's population? It would be just as smart! To the west, the English; to the east, the Québécois. Between the two, a trickle of Israelites.*

Lebeuf closed his copybook. *Do away with ideas. Completely. No generalizations. One scene and then another. Concrete stuff. That's what you need. Nothing else.* Yes, but he had already tried that, and the results had been nil. He was convinced of that. *If only I had a guide, some trustworthy critic. You can never judge yourself.* The man felt despair settle over him. He hunched over and covered his face with his hands. How would he get out of this? Would he have to dive in head first, blindly, like a bull; write anything until he was exhausted? Even that would be better than marking time the way he was doing now... His fist came pounding down on the copybook. *Yet I've got something to say. Why did I leave Boston, then start studying at the time when most were finishing university? Why am I working on those streetcars now if I have nothing going for me.* Was that not proof? Could one fool himself to such a degree? *If only some incentive came from my milieu! If someone would give me some encouragement! But then, people would say that I'd let myself be influenced...*

Lebeuf picked up his pen and copybook, running his hand over the fine paper several times. *In the end something's got to click.* But he did not write anything. Soon he raised his head to look at the clock. *Already nine-thirty!* It was too late to go to the lectures. *Another morning down the drain.* He pulled his notebook out of the drawer to have a look at his "psychological profiles" and became absorbed in reading. *There are some good comments, striking sketches, a certain life.* It was only a matter of fitting all that together, of setting the sketches in motion. *If I only had command of my plot, then it would work.* It suddenly dawned on him that last year he had leafed through a booklet entitled "Plots of 100 Best Novels." *That's what I need.* At the time he had feared that foreknowledge of the plots might spoil his reading. That seemed of no importance to him now. *Go over those plots, mark off the intrigues, arrange for some interesting developments. That's the solution.* He got up in a hurry and pulled a shirt out of his dresser. *Why didn't I think of this before? I've lost a whole year through my own fault.*

XVIII

Suddenly, Lebeuf stood still and cocked an ear. Had he not heard a knock? He started toward the door, but then changed his mind. Who could be showing up this morning? Margot was supposed to come in only around four o'clock. Jules looked through the drawers for a pair of socks. *Where in hell did Margot stuff them?* He was pulling at yet another drawer when three loud knocks sounded unmistakably at the door. He flung his shirt on the chair in a fit of temper. If it was the janitor, she would get a piece of his mind. He had told her before not to disturb him before noon. Without even slipping his robe on, he peeked through the partly opened door.

"Gisèle! What are you doing here?" The thought that Bill had had an accident crossed his mind.

"I'm sorry, I... I just have to see you, Mr. Lebeuf."

"Bill's not sick, is he?"

"No."

"Well then, just a minute, I'll put something on..."

Gisèle remained alone in the dark hallway; she was tempted to run away. The approach, which a moment ago had seemed so adroit, now appeared sure to fail. Looking up a stranger in his home this way! Still she stood motionless in the hall, her heart beating hard, her hands moist. It was best to get things straight now once and for all.

Last night, after the "exam," Gisèle had been overcome with despair. Everything was lost, and by her own fault! She had made the blunder of indicating she did not

103

read much! What conclusion could Lebeuf draw from that? Small wonder he had immediately got up and left. Then, to add the finishing touch, she had declared she would run away from home! *I spoiled everything by a stupid fit.* Right at that moment she had conceived the idea of seeing Lebeuf before he had a chance to talk with her father.

Hidden in her parents' room, she had waited for the guests to leave and had sneaked outside unnoticed. She had followed Jules and Marguerite. *As soon as he takes her back home, I'll go up to Mr. Lebeuf's* she had thought. The shadowing had been made easier by the fact that the couple had decided to walk home. Gisèle's plan seemed the most natural thing to do; she just had to see Lebeuf that very evening. Nothing would make her change her idea. Nothing? After following them from a distance up to Saint Denis Street, Gisèle had seen Jules and Margot enter a big gray house with green cloth awnings. Shivering, she had huddled in a store entrance, sure that the student would soon come out again. How long had she waited thus? One, perhaps two hours? She did not know. Neither did she try to reason out why Lebeuf had walked into Marguerite's and not come out again. Finally both cold and weariness had triumphed over her determination. She had walked back home.

In the morning, she had taken her books as usual, but, instead of heading for school, she had gone back to her observation post at the entrance of the store. A few minutes later, she had seen Marguerite coming out. After waiting a little longer, she had made up her mind to knock at Lebeuf's door. She was still shivering at the thought of her brazenness when the door opened for a second time. The student beckoned her to come in.

He looked as if he were completely over his surprise. His massive face with the flattened nose betrayed no feeling. "Sit down," he said, "and tell me what's happening."

He placed himself in front of her and waited. Gisèle was biting her lips. She had put no lipstick on today, and her long black hair fell in curls over her shoulders, as when she returned from the grocery store the previous evening.

"Mr. Lebeuf, what I said last night isn't true. I... I wouldn't run away from home if..."

"Oh?" Jules ran his hand across his chin. "Still you had thought about it, right?"

Gisèle nodded, then hesitatingly, "I wouldn't run away... I think I'd get married instead."

"You, you would get married? And who to?" He could not explain why, but the news annoyed him.

"To Paul Létourneau..."

"Paul Létourneau? Who's he? What does he do? Why didn't you... No, don't bother answering, I... Do you love him?"

"No, I don't think so."

Lebeuf got up and took a few steps across the room. *Out of sheer spite, she might go ahead with her plan.* "Listen," he said, "maybe there's a way to fix it up."

He started explaining to her that many English students worked part time while taking courses. Why couldn't she follow their example? That way Bill wouldn't have to pay anything. A few years of English would not hurt her. Sir George Williams was considered a good college. That way she would have a chance to try out her aptitude in mathematics. Jules knew a fellow who had registered there the previous year.

Gisèle was all ears. She had never dreamed of such an arrangement. The prospect of finding herself in an English environment frightened her a bit. But there were some advantages.

105

"You think I could find a job working in an office?"

Lebeuf ran his hand through his brush-cut hair. "That is a problem of course."

A sixteen-year-old girl, with no experience, who knew only French. And a part-time job to boot. Where to inquire? Jules could not think of anyone. "That's a problem..."

Unexpectedly, Jules smiled. Sillery! Why not? His father ran his own brokerage and insurance office on Saint James Street. Quite an operation, according to rumor. Augustin acted like a real boor during conversations, but Jules knew that he lent money left and right without ever asking for it back. Surely it was worth trying.

The big man sat back in front of Gisèle. Counseling and protecting her gave him a strange feeling of satisfaction. "Listen, I've got a friend, a student who might be able to help us. Anyway, it doesn't cost anything to try."

Lebeuf went to get his jacket in the closet.

"Right away?" asked Gisèle, her eyes bright with excitement.

"We'll give it a try. If we can't find him, we can always go for a coffee together; I haven't had breakfast."

He had a peek at his watch: ten-fifty. No doubt Augustin could be found at the Venus, a café on Phillips Square. That was where the student would settle after a session at the Two-Bit and his night-time ramblings. *It's the work of the devil if this morning for once he has decided to go to the university.*

XIX

Lebeuf was right. Walking into the Venus, he spotted Sillery sitting at a table in the back, a glass of wine in his hand. He must have been up all night. His shiny eyes and pale complexion were sure signs of long wakefulness.

"I have a little wild flower for you, dear friend," said Lebeuf.

Augustin seemed delighted to see them. "Oh idyllic couple, sprung for my delight from the outside gloom! Oh *licet*, I shall protect her like a rose in my own garden."

"Gisèle Lafrenière, Augustin Sillery," said Lebeuf. The young girl self-consciously stammered some greeting.

Augustin seemed delighted to see them. "O idyllic couple, sprung for my delight from the outside gloom! O couple, be seated, may you be my guests."

Glancing at Lebeuf, Gisèle sat down on the imitation leather seat.

"And now," said Augustin, "let's get down to serious business. *Ita est*, the gruelling chore of finding a nectar worthy of cooling the pink lips of..."

"What will you have?" Lebeuf asked the young girl.

Gisèle was doing her best to look at ease, but the luxurious restaurant as well as the student's incomprehensible words and Parisian accent totally intimidated her. She appeared to become engrossed in reading the menu, on which were listed dishes and courses and drinks she had never seen.

"I think I'll have a chocolate milk shake." At least she knew what that was.

Sillery snapped his fingers for the waitress. "Miss, take this poisoned cup from me," he gestured toward his glass of port, "and fetch forthwith two milk chocolates on the rocks."

"Rum coffee and toast," said Lebeuf.

Once the waitress had served them, the big man began to explain the purpose of his visit. Without dwelling on the money question, he let Augustin in on the situation. He even let it be understood that the Lafrenières did not condone their daughter's plans, but that Gisèle had made up her mind that she would free herself. Sillery was observing him with piercing eyes.

"So then, as I know that your father does business in town, I thought that maybe you could give us a hand."

After he had made sure that it was not a joke, Augustin appeared to be thinking it over. A thousand thoughts were running through his mind at once. He had not set foot in his house during the last three days, and when he showed up again he could expect a thundering blast from his father. Would not turning up at his father's office "on business" be the best way to restrain him to silence? Mr. Sillery would never dare resort to abusive language in the presence of a stranger. If, as was possible, the businessman turned down his request, Augustin would still have the pleasure of telling his mother about the scene, underscoring the tragic situation the "poor young girl" was faced with and how she burst into tears on her way out of the office. Mrs. Sillery would take care of the rest. Caught up in his thoughts, Sillery was scratching his head, somewhat perplexed. Lebeuf almost regretted asking for a favor that caused so much trouble.

"Please, do not interpret my silence as a sign of hesitation," said Sillery finally. "Yet, as I am not exactly in my

108

noble sire's good graces, I am thinking about the best strategy to follow…''

"If it's too much of a problem," said Jules, "we can try something else."

"Not at all." Sillery had a sip of his milk shake and put it down with a wince. "Not at all. Stimulated by this ambrosian drink and emboldened by the eloquent words the presence of our charming guest will not fail to inspire, I shall proceed toward my father's dwelling and tell him 'Father, I have fished from the limpid waters of this our metropolis this dazzling pearl!'' He gestured histrionically toward Gisèle who was listening to him, her mouth half open. '' 'Let us not sweep her under the carpet. Let us employ her. Let us make her bear fruit so that…''

"Yeah," interrupted Lebeuf, "you think it's gonna work?"

'' 'To conquer without peril…' '' With another wince, Augustin dipped his lips into his shake, then stretched out hir arm. "May this milky toast, gulped under the sign of Venus," he was pointing to the painted silhouette of a woman on the wall "influence the fates in a way favorable to the homeric plans we embrace." He had one more sip. "And now, 'it's time, let's pull up anchor,' en route! I'm sorry, my dear Lebeuf, not to be able to invite you as a member of my retinue, but, as you know, certain deeds are better performed by two than by three."

Jules gestured as if to hold Sillery back, but Gisèle had already risen to follow Augustin. The big man saw Sillery opening the door solemnly, letting the young woman go ahead, then hailing a cab on Saint Catherine Street.

Part Two

I

A flower in his buttonhole, a cigarette holder between his teeth, Sillery was pacing to and fro between the Church of Saint James and the corner of Saint Catherine Street. Memories of the day's events were dizzily whirling in his head. As he walked, expressions of his inner turmoil came out in brusque and nervous gestures that caused passersby to turn around.

First, he relived the interview with his father, at the office, where Gisèle had gotten the job... Things had gone well at first. Mr. Sillery, although rather surprised by the proceedings had been proper, almost calm. After greeting Augustin coldly, he had asked Gisèle some questions, gone out a few moments to consult with his office manager, then had returned to announce he could hire the young woman from the beginning of the holidays, as she wished. Once she had gotten used to the office routine, she could continue as a part-time employee from September on. The ease with which Mr. Sillery had granted the request appeared suspicious to Augustin. *Careful! There's a snake in the grass!*

He was not wrong. Just as he was getting up to walk Gisèle to the door — after many profuse thanks — his father had held him back. "Stay a while, I've got to talk to you."

His father's voice was calm, slightly sad. Tensed up but appearing placid, Augustin had taken a seat facing the massive desk with its thick glass plate. A long, oppressive silence had followed. He could hear the clattering of typewriters and the muffled ringing of telephones from behind the door.

"Listen, Augustin." There was a quiver in his father's voice. He had to make a great effort to control himself. "We... you and I often had differences of opinion. I believed for a long time that it was your fault, that if you'd wanted... to make concessions, we could have a normal relationship as father and son..."

Mr. Sillery had grabbed hold of the letter opener and was tapping it against his knee. *What's with him?* Augustin had difficulty breathing and felt slightly dizzy. *Stay calm, no fainting here.*

"Now I'm not so sure about that," continued Mr. Sillery. "Maybe it's a question of a conflict of personalities that we can do nothing about." The businessman lowered his head and laid the letter opener back on his desk, gently, as if it were a delicate and important operation. His face — round, yet firmly chiseled — was less florid than usual, his beady gray eyes, less piercing.

The tone in his voice changed abruptly. "But that's not why I kept you here. I'm in good health. I've got my work. I can manage and so can you, I presume?"

Was he expecting a response? Augustin stopped smoking. "Perfectly well, thank you."

"So much the better," answered Mr. Sillery," so much the better..." Reaching for his letter opener, he began to wave it with the tip of his fingers. Then suddenly he leaned his elbow against the desk and staring straight at his son he said, "But your mother, she's sick. She had an attack last night. We had to call for a doctor."

Augustin felt a cold sweat cover his entire body. *It's all over* he thought. *It had to happen,* not knowing very well what he meant by that. He opened his mouth to speak, but suddenly he was overwhelmed and broke into sobs. His eyes filled with tears. Quickly, he coughed hard, then clutched his handkerchief as if he wanted to clear a frog from his throat. *How sick is she? Did he notice me?* Both these questions darted simultaneously across his mind.

Mr. Sillery stared blankly at his paper knife for a while before he added, "Small wonder, anyway. Sleeping two hours a night, eating like a bird, drinking one cup of tea after another. God, what a life!"

Augustin bit his lips to restrain the tears. What a pathetically dull life, indeed, Mrs. Sillery led as she spent most of her time with her Chinese tea, alone, especially at night, in the large dining room surrounded by her oak furniture and novels. *It's all over; it just had to happen.*

Augustin cleared his throat to make sure that he could talk. "Is she in danger?"

"Fortunately no. It's not critical yet. If she takes it easy, has some rest and peace of mind, she'll be able to pull out of it..."

Augustin gritted his teeth. *He did that on purpose, he exaggerated the whole thing to see what my reaction would be.* The student was just burning to question him further so as to know what to think and get more details. But he refrained. *He would be all too happy to see that I am "punished."* His mother was not in a critical state and that was the important thing. "Well then, thank you for the information. I'll probably see her this evening."

Mr. Sillery gestured as if he meant to keep him a while longer, but he let his hand drop. "Don't mention it."

Without looking back, Augustin dashed out of the office. He was choking. He had a lump in his throat. A minute more of this and he would have burst into tears amid the indifferent employees tapping away on their machines. As he reached the door, someone stood up and blocked his way.

113

"Thank you very much for what you've done, Mr Sillery." Augustin looked. It was Gisèle. He had forgotten she even existed.

"It's quite all right — the least I could do."

Should he say good-bye to her now? He wavered. No, her company was better than solitude. "Let's go. I'll drive you back home."

Augustin bumped against a passerby and suddenly remembered where he was: Saint Denis Street. *I should get home now, mother's sick.* How often had he paced between the Church of Saint James and the corner of Saint Catherine? He could not tell. His cigarette had burned itself out at the tip of his ivory holder. He consulted his watch. *Eight-ten. Another twenty minutes and I'll go.*

Augustin resumed his walk and, once more, the events of the day flooded his brain... He had accompanied Gisèle back home in a cab. They had chatted along the way. She was not an unpleasant girl — clean, natural, pretty... She had told him a little of her life — her simple schoolgirl worries, her ambitions, the satisfaction she derived from the prospect of paying her own way through school. The chat had given Augustin a reprieve. Life was so simple for some people!

But the truce had been short. Once Gisèle had left, Augustin had again been faced with his anguish. *What have I done? I'm not responsible for my mother's sickness after all!* For a minute, he had been quite determined to go home and see her right away. But after riding for a few more minutes, he had asked the cabbie to please drive him to the La Salle Hotel. *A fit of tears would only make things worse.*

He had rented a room, showered, taken two tranquilizers, then gone to bed. Seven hours he had slept, seven

114

hours straight. A deep, dreamless sleep. Waking up, he had wondered where he was. Right away he had remembered and had thought of going home. He had had the bellhop bring him up a steak, done rare, and a shirt. The one he had was wrinkled and stank of sweat. *It's because of the interview with father at the office...* He had taken another shower, cold this time, wolfed down his steak and dressed with care. *I must go home.* He had spent a long time sitting still in an armchair by the window, pondering. Suddenly, around seven-thirty, he had left the hotel, almost at a run, and jumped onto a streetcar.

And now, he was here stupidly pacing up and down Saint Denis in front of the Super Restaurant. *I'll wait till precisely eight-thirty; then I'll go.* Why eight-thirty? Why not eight-twenty-five or eight-forty? *Crazy.* Augustin lit a cigarette. *Anyway, I only have fifteen minutes left to wait...*

He was suddenly attracted by what was going on nearby. Two young fellows were talking animatedly at the entrance of a bowling alley. They looked as if they would come to blows any moment now. Some pedestrians had stopped to see how the argument would end. One of the antagonists was accusing the other of having trumped up the score so as to pocket the wager money. The second fellow, lank and restless looking, objected vehemently. In the end, despite encouragement from some bystanders to fight it out, they separated, bad mouthing each other. The crowd dispersed. But Augustin, fascinated, remained there motionless, feet glued to the ground, in front of the stairwell leading up to the bowling alley. The thundering roll of the balls on the wooden floor upstairs and the banging of the wooden pins tumbling on the padded endwall of the alley could be heard. During his endless walks up and down Saint Denis, the student had often passed in front of this entrance. Without paying too much

115

attention to it, he had noticed quite a few youths, in groups of two, three of four, going up the steps. His heart missed a beat. *Could that be why?* He looked at the time. *Another twelve minutes.* He watched for a long time in front of the Super Restaurant — "Canadian Cooking and Others" — then suddenly straightened his bow tie, and started up the stairs.

II

Mathieu Bowling Alleys looked like all the bowling establishments Augustin had seen before. To the left, by the wall, a stand for cigarettes, soft drinks and candies was also used as cashier's counter where a big, jowly type, in a soft flannel shirt, was enthroned. To the right, twelve parallel alleys, made of sanded maple, with triangles of pins under a green-shaded light at the end. The pin boys sat on the dividing walls between the ends of the alleys. On either side of the alleys ran a gutter for stray balls. All alleys, save the third one — doubtless where the argument of a while back had started — were taken, Augustin took a deep breath and checked the position of his tie; then bright and watchful, he made his way toward the right, apologizing each time he passed in front of a player. The thought of his mother skipped through his mind. He repressed it impatiently. *I am not up to it now. I must calm down first.* Augustin stopped when he reached the seventh track. It was taken by three players, two male teenagers and a young woman. The girl was hardly older than her mates — eighteen or twenty, she was short and heavy set, plump, her breasts well outlined by her green sweater. Sillery despised her at first sight. *An animal for breeding.* On the other hand, one of the young men was interesting. Blond, slim, lithe, with sinuous muscles, he had a lock of sweat-soaked hair that curled down over his forehead. The other man was insignificant — a small, thick, swarthy type who carried himself like a gorilla.

The game was drawing to a close. The scoresheet showed that the last round was coming up. They were good players; no doubt they played regularly. Bending forward, almost squatting, the swarthy one had a smile of triumph on his lips as he watched the pins at the other end of the alley go flying, making him the winner. The blond type dabbed the sweat from his brow, looking vexed.

Sillery walked up to the blond youth and spoke loudly so that all would hear. "Excuse me, sir. I see that the game is over and that there are only three of you. I was supposed to meet friends here tonight. They were held up at the last minute. So, I thought that perhaps you would allow me to join you..."

All three looked at one another with surprise. Sillery had neither the look nor the dress of a bowler. After eyeing him from head to foot, the young lady turned her back on him, took out her compact and touched up her makeup. The dark-haired one seemed indecisive. "You know how to play?" he asked.

"Very little, unfortunately. I've played only three or four times. But," Augustin added quickly, "I'm really enormously interested in it."

"Losers pay, yuh know."

"Quite all right with me. You have to pay something to learn anything."

The dark fellow consulted his girl friend with a look, and she shrugged indifferently. The blond, still smarting over his defeat, was going over the scoresheet with an air of humiliation.

"All right then, you start first," said the swarthy youth. "You can put yer suit jacket on that bench over there. We'll let you start."

Augustin went to get rid of his jacket. He was overcome by a stange sense of excitement. *Alea jacta est* he said to himself with glee, not knowing too well what he meant. He strutted back to the alley.

In her large, grade-school handwriting, the teenaged girl was writing the names of the players down. After having asked Augustin twice to spell his name, she wrote down C-E-L-E-R-Y and looked at him to make sure it was really correct.

"Perfect, miss, perfect. They always say my name sounds like a hors d'oeuvre; I was never made so sure of it as now."

But the girl was not listening. She was engrossed in the writing down of her own name, M-U-R-I-E-L-L-E.

"Do you often come and play here?" inquired Augustin.

"Now and then, often enough, I guess. Not too often. Sometimes I come around three times a week."

"Three times a week!" exclaimed Augustin, as he took a quick look at the blond adolescent, who was busy talking with his dark friend a few feet away. "Very interesting! No wonder then you're so superbly developed."

Murielle gave him a side glance, and, not knowing what to answer, she proceeded to write down the other names, G-A-S-T-O-N and H-E-N-R-I. The way she bent over to write made her backside balloon out under her too-tight skirt. *And to think that some men would actually find that provocative.* He felt envious of them.

The two teenagers had ended their discussion. They drew closer to check on the intruder's ability. Augustin clumsily grabbed both balls and threw them consecutively, without aiming. The first one rolled off the alley before reaching the pins, while the second barely hit one pin on the left corner.

With an air of satisfaction, Henri elbowed his fairhaired friend. It was the latter's turn. Looking solemn, he took

119

the ball in his hand, approached the alley and swept all the pins down in one shot. He pulled up his pants with a quick twist of the wrist as he looked for Murielle's reaction.

Augustin came close to the young man and casually put his hand over his arm. "But dear me, what remarkable skill!"

Gaston turned around surprised. Sillery had been miles from his mind. The student felt a twinge in the pit of his stomach. *What am I doing in this place throwing these ridiculous balls? Mother is home waiting for me. It's time to go.*

"I really don't know how you do it. Is it hard?"

Gaston repressed a self-satisfied smile. *Flattery always works at first* thought Augustin. *If only the rest was as easy!*

"How do I do it? Not hard." Gaston picked up a ball. "Yuh take the ball this way, yuh see? Thumb in this here hole, an' yer two other fingers in the other two holes, yuh see?"

"I see."

"Then yuh throw it out this way." Gaston got ready. "Yer lef' foot forward. If yer lef' foot's not up there, yer aim's no good."

"Really interesting!"

Gaston's biceps were flexing beautifully under the pale copper hairs of his skin. Sillery would have liked to pinch them, bite into them.

"That's not all. When you're set this way, yuh gotta give it a twist o' the wrist, like this to give yer ball a curve so that it strikes the front pin at an angle. That's when yuh get'em. Bang! Not one left, yuh see?"

Gaston put the ball back in the gutter and pulled up his pants. "That's all there is to it."

Augustin's eyes lit up. "Such precision! Advanced ballistics!" Augustin caught hold of himself; learned

120

terms invariably produced a bad effect. "I mean, you made me think of a professional baseball player."

But Henri was getting a bit impatient. How could his apprentice be asked instead of him. And Gaston was swaggering around that effeminate character who could not even throw a ball down the alley.

"Come on, are we playin' bowling or not? This ain't a school here. We're not gonna start givin' lessons to everybody."

Augustin felt stung to the quick. Was this runt going to jeopardize his efforts? "Of course not," he answered in his falsetto tone. "Not hard to see right away that you could not give anybody lessons in anything, especially not in good manners."

His remarks were above Henri's head, but it was clear to him that "Celery" had meant to insult him. He decided to get really mad. "What do you mean by that? I don't take wisecracks like that."

"Well, that's curious!" Augustin was now feeling in complete command of himself. If this fellow wanted a fight, why not? He felt capable of toppling that little ape in a jiffy. "Funny enough! You have a yap that could gulp down anything, even garter snakes."

Bothered and a trifle surprised at the quickness and sharpness of the comeback, Henri clenched his fists and walked toward Sillery menacingly. "I'm gonna show yuh who can gulp anything!"

Murielle placed herself between the pair. "Come on Ti-ri, take it easy now! Let him play. You're the one who started it."

Henri seemed satisfied with that. He let Murielle lead him aside, though he growled a little. Honor had been saved.

Augustin picked up his balls, ignoring Gaston, as if the incident had been unimportant to him. He chanced a ball and managed to strike down three pins.

Gaston moved close to him. "That's better than before. But yuh still don't have the right twist of the wrist."

Augustin held back a smile of triumph. "I'm rather bad. We'll have to get together here alone one of these nights. Then you could have all the time you need to teach me the tricks of the trade."

Gaston appeared embarrassed. He gave the others a shy glance. "Yeah, maybe. But all three of us come here together, yuh know."

He hardly opened his mouth as he spoke and his voice was soft. Augustin moved away a few feet so that Gaston would follow him. *That funky kid.* The finding of his weakness only aggravated his desire.

"I see," he whispered. "Murielle is your girl friend, isn't she?"

"No, Murielle's not my girl."

There was irritation in the boy's voice. It became clear to Sillery that he had just touched a sensitive spot. Some rivalry must exist between Gaston and Henri. And Murielle was apparently giving preference to Henri.

"Then could it be that you'd be afraid to displease Henri?" insinuated Augustin. "He doesn't seem to be the most even-tempered guy around."

Gaston made a gesture as if to warn Augustin not to speak so loudly. Then all of a sudden he got mad. "I go out with who I want, that's all."

"As you wish."

Augustin shrugged and walked closer to the alley just as Murielle made a double strike.

"Good for you! An excellent shot. It's rare to find skill and beauty in one and the same person."

Flushing with delight, Murielle giggled. *What a ridiculous chick!* Henri was keeping a hostile eye on the whole scene. Gaston stepped up to play his turn. He got set, aimed with care, threw his two balls in a row; three pins stayed in the alley. Simulating indifference, he went back to the scoresheet where Augustin and Murielle sat.

"I slipped," he said. "That's why I missed my shot."

He was not addressing either one in particular. He was only talking for relief. *The soul of a child who does not deserve his beauty* thought Sillery. He suddenly thought of his mother. Was it possible for him to neglect her for a stranger? *I must go home.* But as he was turning around to leave, he noticed Gaston coming toward him. A shiver of pleasure ran through him.

"Listen, I thought about... 'bout what yuh said earlier. Think I've got nothin' to do on Monday night."

"Monday night? Let's see now," said Augustin.

He felt a welling up of joy. *Easy now.* "Just a minute, let me check my diary here... Monday night, let's see now... Yes, I think it would be all right. As long as it's not too early. Say between nine and nine-thirty?"

"Okay. Nine o'clock I'll be here."

Gaston seemed in a hurry to finish the conversation.

"So then, let me jot it down here. Mathieu Alleys, nine o'clock. Maybe we could go and have a drink to cool off after the game?"

Gaston made a gesture of indecision. Augustin bit his lips. *Not so fast, stupid!* But it was too late to back out. "Unless you never touch spirits? Maybe they make you sick?"

Gaston tugged at his pants and with cockiness answered, "Sick? No way. I can hold my booze as well as anybody else."

"All right then, I'll be here on Monday."

Augustin took a deep breath, his nostrils quivering, and walked toward the alley to pick up his balls with a triumphant air.

III

All the sweepers of the Hochelaga section were in a state of excitement. Gathered in their lunch shack, they were animatedly debating the event of the day. Bouboule had just been fired! The cause — he had struck Lévêque on the head with his broom the night before in a fit of anger. Two other sweepers had had to intervene to quiet the old man, who had wanted to settle his accounts once and for all with those "good-for-nothing, arse-lickers of big shots." Hadn't Lévêque had the gall to come right out and say that Bouboule was doing a lousy job?

The sweepers' opinions varied on the incident. They all agreed that Lévêque was a bastard, and they were happy that Bouboule had had the nerve to face up to him. Some, however, thought that the old man had acted too roughly.

But it was the company's decision which had stirred up their most violent reaction. Of course the management could not close its eyes on such an incident. If it had contented itself with suspending Bouboule for a month or two, no one would have protested. But it had purely and simply fired him without pension benefits, and granted him only six months' severance pay.

What could they do about it anyway? Nobody had yet risked a suggestion.

"The whole bloody thing stinks," said Charlot. "After working thirty years for this company..."

The others nodded their approval.

"An old man like him who lives all by himself..."

"Yeah," said Bill. "Don't as' me what he's gonna do now. Over sixty years old, no job, completely washed out. An' on top of that, he's far from being rich. He spends his time, every goddamn evening the Lord spares him, playin' cards with his chums. Let me tell yuh that he gets wiped out clean. The poor bugger can't even tell the difference between spades and clubs." Bill had come to this conclusion after the card party held at his house. "So it's clear and simple: he's out on his arse, poor as Job."

"I wouldn't say he's out on his arse. That's a bit too much," said Marceau, a big sweeper with wobbly cheeks and tearful eyes. "He's not rich, all right, but flat-out broke, well, I don't know 'bout that. He still has a house after all, hasn't he?"

Indignant, Bill turned to Marceau. "A house? Goddamn! Yuh call that a house! When yuh see that house of his?"

Marceau shook his head negatively.

"I'd like yuh to go an' have a look at it! Christ! Yuh can see all the lathes on the ceiling, an' when yuh walk on the bloody floors, hell, you're scared to end up in the bloody cellar each step yuh take. A house? Well I don't call that a house, I call it a shack."

The other sweepers remained pensive. Even the cashier, who had stuck his big, shiny, bald head through the wicket, did not feel like joking. He had known Bouboule for twenty-two years. For twenty-two years, six times a week, he had seen him there on that maple bench — made shiny by the rubbing of overalls. He had a lump in his throat just looking at that empty space today.

The clock in the large room struck four times. Lunch hour had long been over. But none of the sweepers was thinking of getting up. The rest they were taking tonight at the company's expense was a kind of revenge. And also a sort of tribute to Bouboule, that slightly ridiculous old man who had shown the courage of his convictions by hitting authority smack in the face. Besides, the sweepers were at ease: Lévêque, with a bandage over his eye, would not dare show up.

Charlot, looking torn by some inner struggle, was growing fidgety on his bench. He suddenly decided to speak up. "Dammit boys, wouldn't it be possible to do something about it?"

There was a glimmer of hope. All eyes turned to him. Lebeuf himself was scrutinizing him hard with special interest. Since the beginning, he had waited to hear such a comment, but he would not have made it himself, fearing to arouse a feeling of animosity in Charlot and a few other old-timers. He was only a newcomer after all.

"We're behind yuh, Charlot," Marceau said with unusual warmth. "One hundred percent. Just say the word. We're behind yuh."

"No doubt about it, we're behind yuh." continued Bill approvingly. "But, hell, what can we do? If yuh wanna have a collection, well I'm not rich but I'll be the first one to throw in a five."

The rest of them grunted approvingly. Charlot was scratching his head. "It's all very nice to make a collection. I'm not against it. But it wouldn't solve the problem, not one bit."

The silence in the shack grew heavy. Charlot was right.

Isn't he going to come out with a concrete suggestion? thought Lebeuf. But Charlot seemed resolved not to add anything. He had done his share.

The student finally decided to say something. "Perhaps we could go and see Stevens?"

The sweepers looked at him with a mixture of apprehension and admiration. Lebeuf saw that Charlot agreed.

126

Stevens was the head of all the company's hired hands, the boss you saw only once a year during the inspection round. Yet, the older employees remembered that he, too, had started off as a sweeper, some thirty years back. In the beginning, after his first promotion, it had still been possible to talk to him. He had showed up often enough. He would come and exchange a few words with his former colleagues. Then he had received other promotions. The company had developed. Stevens had provided himself with assistants — Riley and Durand. Now he was unapproachable. Had he given the orders on this matter or had one of his assistants been overzealous? No one knew. But head and assistants were all perceived with the same mistrust and the same unspoken hostility.

It came to Lebeuf that his companions' attitude was both shy and dead set. *Obviously* he thought. *Obviously, they're afraid.* For a moment he felt annnoyed, almost angry. Why were they so down at the mouth? Why did they not get organized? Why did they not demand higher wages? But irritation suddenly receded. *What would I do* he went on thinking *if I was the one who had a wife and kids and had worked here for ten, twenty, thirty years, if I only had to sit it out for a few years before getting my pension — or lose it by merely one act of insubordination?*

One of the sweepers had finally decided to speak his mind. "Yeah well, any guy who'd go and see Stevens about this would run the risk of getting shafted like Bouboule."

"You're not serious?" asked Lebeuf. "Going to see the boss isn't the same as hitting someone over the..."

Big Marceau interrupted him earnestly. "It's been seen before, Lebeuf, it's been seen before. Ask the others. I'm not blaming yuh now. Yuh're new here. Yuh ain't seen what we seen. It would happen slowly but surely. First, maybe they'd start by transferring the guy. They'd put

127

him on the tracks in winter, puttin' salt and cleanin' switches like a beginner. And they would keep an eye on him. Maybe they'd leave him alone if he watched himself. Maybe too they'd catch him warmin' up in a restaurant 'cause the guy's frozen in winter. Then, so long friend, yuh wouldn't ever hear of him again. We've seen that before…''

"Yeah!"

Lebeuf scratched his head. He was thinking about his interview with Riley the previous winter. The bosses had wanted to make the sweepers shovel snow. He had won his point that time. But he hesitated to mention it now. He did not want to give the impression that he was bragging. But finally he made up his mind to get it off his chest. There was no way they could let Bouboule down. "Yeah well, you'll remember, Marceau, that last winter I went to head office with Bouboule and nothing happened, but in the end we weren't shoveling snow."

Marceau did not appear impressed at all. "All right, we didn't shovel any snow. But Bouboule's not around any more either. Lévêque was always on his back. They left *you* alone, but I don't know why. Or rather, maybe I do know why. Lévêque's scared o' you. He's shittin' in his pants, 'specially since you slapped that driver down when he sideswiped you with his car 'cause he thought you weren't gettin' out o' the way fast enough. Lévêque was there, you remember…''

Lebeuf had forgotten that incident.

"Well you'd better watch out," concluded Marceau, "watch out. Maybe you don't mind losing your job. But I'd say you're on shaky ground."

All the sweepers agreed on that. Why had Lebeuf not received a warning before this time? *Maybe they want to get rid of me.* Maybe the sweepers thought giving him a warning would not change his attitude.

"Well, that's another matter," said Jules. "Today we're talking about Bouboule. What do you think, Charlot? You're the one who talked first."

The Italian contorted his monkey face. Marceau's words had brought him back to the real situation. "What do I think of it? Same as everyone."

Lebeuf did not try to hide his despair. If nobody was behind him, there was no use in going to the head office.

Bill suddenly erupted, his lower jaw trembling, his face grimacing with indignation. "Yuh want me to tell yuh, boys, what our trouble is, goddammit! Our problem is that from first to last, startin' with me, we're shittin' in our pants 'cause we're afraid to lose our li'l jobs! But last winter, Bouboule — he might not know the difference between clubs and spades, but he's not that dumb — last winter, Jesus Christ, when he went to the head office with Lebeuf he knew what he was doin' an' he went just the same. An' now that he's flat out are we gonna leave him there, flat out for Chrissake, without lifting a finger? Are yuh gonna be shit on by the bosses every day in yer life and say 'thank you, very nice o' you?' Holy Jesus, we've gotta sink or swim. I'm behind yuh a hundred percent, Lebeuf. We gotta do something!"

The sweepers' opinions switched completely around. "You're right."

"We've been shit on long enough!"

"Goddamned Lévêque's through with running us around like sheep."

Fists were clenched. Some wanted to strike right away, to march on the head office.

Seeing how things were turning out, the jowly cashier shut the wicket and went back to his accounts. It was surely going to end badly. And he was not a sweeper after all. *If they question me, I haven't heard anything.*

Charlot, for one, seemed to have come to terms with the

situation. It was too late to back out. It was a matter of not losing their cool and of going about it systematically. "Listen boys, let's not go off half-cocked. We've got to go to the head office all right, but not all at once, and not only one of us either. We've got to send a delegation."

"Yuh're right," said Bill. "Yuh go with Lebeuf then."

Approving grunts were heard from all sides of the room. Charlot brought a finger to his scowling face. "Yuh know I don't speak English, boys."

"Lebeuf can translate," retorted Marceau. "And anyway, Stevens knows French, I heard him once with Lévêque one time he came here."

"All right then, I've nothing else to say. But," he pointed out, raising his hand in a plea for silence, "we'll need an old worker with us, an old timer who's known Bouboule from the start, and who's also known Stevens. Whaddya say yuh come along, Pop Breton?"

Old Breton, a small taciturn type with a tawny complexion and a bony face like an old Indian, wiggled his lower jaw sporadically, as if he had lost his power of speech. His quick beady eyes were rolling in their sockets like those of a trapped animal. "I have only one year to go before I hit my pension."

His reply was met by a thunder of protest. Pop Breton passed for a rich man. His miserly ways had become legendary.

"Nothin' but one short year." He already saw himself ruined, penniless, begging for a living. His brown complexion blushed with red blotches.

"And Bouboule, how long did he have to go?"

"And what about Bouboule, how long did he have to go? Can't just think only about yourself, Pop. You've got to be sensible about it," declared big Marceau, impassively.

130

The old man's jaws waggled once more. He had nothing to say to counter that. That Bouboule was a hot head, well, that was for sure. If he had kept quiet, as he himself had, the whole thing would not have happened. But they had worked together for nearly twenty years. Things like that you could not change; things like that mattered. "All right, good enough," he finally answered in his raspy voice. "If that's the way it is, I'll go."

The old man got up as if he had to leave right away. Charlot had to explain to him that the delegation was not going to the head office until ten o'clock and that he would have to put on his Sunday clothes.

IV

Sillery had a look at his watch: four-thirty. He had left the bowling alley at eleven-forty-five, firmly intending to go home. But first he had stopped over at a café on Saint Lawrence Street "just to relax a little." His argument with Henri and his ribbing of Gaston had shaken him... After sipping two scotches, he had noticed that the clock read twelve-forty-five. *Mother must be in bed. I can't go in now.* So he would have to wait till the wee hours of the morning to be sure to see Mrs. Sillery alone in the dining room, as usual... if, by any chance, she could get up. *I knew it would happen.*

He had walked over to a bar on Clark Street, where most of the customers were Chinese and which was open illegally all night. There Sillery had started talking with an ex-merchant whom the Japanese had forced to flee Peking in 1934, leaving his young wife and three children behind. Since then he had been trying to bring them over to Canada, but to no avail. He was existing in Montreal thanks to a small rice, tea and almond business. He was not complaining; if he was separated from his family, no doubt it was because it had to be that way. Augustin listened to him with utmost attention, asking questions and attempting to find out precisely what this man's concept of "destiny" was. Although the Chinese expressed himself in good English and seemed educated enough, the student had not been able to understand him completely. It was not a question of language so much as a question of ways of thinking. The Chinese was a fatalist without being one, or rather he acted as if he was not. He accepted the fact that his thoughts were his own. But in no way did he try to guide them, transform them or further them. What especially struck Augustin was the calm way in which this solitary man, separated from his family, ten thousand miles from his homeland, accepted the tribulations of life without any revolt or any recrimination. *It's not a question of thought. It's a question of temperament, of ethnic conditioning.* Augustin arranged to meet the middle-aged Chinese again on the following Wednesday.

Walking out of the bar, he felt relaxed. The Chinese's attitude had relaxed him. He decided to take a streetcar to his home *so as to arrive at exactly the right time.* While on the streetcar he managed a relative serenity. Each time the thought of his mother would cross his mind, he would push it away. *It's not that bad... I am not responsible... I'll just have to be careful...* Gaston's face appeared in his mind. He pushed it away. *Not now, later on.* The Chinese was the one who made a good subject for meditation; calm, resigned, he let life flow, lost in some kind of a dream. *That was the solution...* But stepping down from the streetcar, he felt uneasy again. *I am now leaving the Orient to enter real life.* His weary eye ran over Snowdon Square. The fellow he thought he had seen the other day, was he keeping watch somewhere? No. The square was deserted. *That same fear again! Because I must meet Gaston again, my nerves are shaken.* He started to run. *I must not think of Gaston. I'll see Mom in a few seconds.* He stopped, inhaled deeply a few times. *Nothing like it to calm your nerves.* His heart was throbbing. His hands felt clammy.

When he arrived at his house, he walked cautiously toward the door, opened it silently. A wave of joy settled

133

over him. In the dimness of the dining room where he could discern the massive oak sideboard, a faint light flickered. Quickly, he tiptoed toward the light. Mrs. Sillery was there, at her usual place at the end of the table, her tea cup curling its ribbon of steam before her. She must have heard her son come in — her eyes were fixed on the door. Augustin thought he noticed a slight swelling on her left cheek; it seemed to stretch upward, and the eye itself did not seem as open as usual. He drew closer to her and kissed her forehead.

"How are you, mother?" he asked very softly.

She lifted her big eyes toward him; they did not have their habitual directness. "Very well, Augustin, and yourself?"

Such a full-toned voice. At least that had not changed.

"So much the better," he said, "so much the better... It's just that Father intimated at the office that... You know what I mean?"

Mrs. Sillery nodded affirmatively. "Well, you know, your father will be frightened by a scratch..." She smiled feebly, which gave her features their usual symmetry. *Maybe I'm mistaken after all* thought Augustin.

"Anyway," continued his mother, "today sickness doesn't exist anymore. I mean suffering. With the drugs and all. Was it not *your* Valéry who said that?"

As a rule, Mrs Sillery read only authors of the past generation. It had been only at Augustin's insistence that she had resigned herself to reading that "decadent."

"If that's all we had to worry about..." She suddenly changed the subject. Augustin must not interpret her words as a reproach. "What you did for that young girl, Gisèle, is very good. I am happy..."

What was Augustin's relationsip with that young woman? "An extremely pretty" young woman, her husband had commented, and he normally did not notice such

134

things. But to her knowledge, it was the first time Augustin had been interested in a young woman.

"Oh, you know, it was just to help her out..." The student regretted the lie. Since his mother never questioned him, he could always tell her the truth.

"She's pretty?"

"Yes."

Mrs. Sillery got up. "I almost forgot to pour you some tea. I wonder where my head is today."

Augustin gestured, as if to assist her, but he remained seated as usual. "Indeed," he replied, "you're neglecting yourself! "

Mrs. Sillery filled the cup and then set the teapot down on the silver tripod. "Where did you meet her?"

"A school colleague. Lebeuf. Remember him?"

"Yes."

"He introduced us."

So it had not been a fortuitous meeting then. Surely a respectable young woman. Poor, of course, since she had to work. But there was nothing wrong with that. Money had no bearing. Mrs. Sillery thought about the dowry she had received when she was married. What had it given her? She never touched that money except to write Augustin a check once in a while. She shook her head. *What's wrong with me? Some young girl I don't know...*

Quickly she changed the subject. "You really should read Loti, you know. You are full of prejudices." The diamond on her long white hand sparkled as she pointed to the book in front of her, *Azyadé*.

"Yes, I'll try one of these days."

This was his mother, the very embodiment of delicacy. A few general questions to show her interest in Gisèle, a friend of her son's, then she would go on to something else, some intellectual subject. If Augustin had been able to meet another woman like his mother, he would have loved her — not physically maybe — but he would have loved her. The student felt his hands turning clammy where he held them under the table. He took out his handkerchief to wipe them.

"They criticize descriptive narrative a lot today," said Mrs. Sillery slowly. "It's out of style, like I am. For instance, I had read narrative descriptions of Europe before going, and then, once I got there..." She gestured her disillusionment.

"It wasn't nice?"

"Oh certainly it was nice, but books are better. Even a mere tourist's guide..." Mrs. Sillery opened her mouth to continue talking, but her expression froze. A sharp, shooting pain the tranquilizers had not alleviated struck below her left breast. *As long as Augustin doesn't notice anything.* "But here I am chatting away! You must be tired?"

"Yes, a bit," he answered getting up. "And you? You're staying up?"

Mrs. Sillery smiled; the attack was over. "Well yes, of course. You know I've got to finish my Loti. It's only the third time that I've read *Azyadé*. I'm just burning to find out the ending."

Once again Augustin placed a kiss on his mother's forehead and went out in a rush. He felt like crying.

V

Lebeuf and Charlot had been waiting an hour, sitting in the anteroom to Mr. Stevens' office. It was ten-fifteen — and old Breton had not showed up yet.

Dressed in a navy-blue serge suit, sitting on the edge of a big, red-leather armchair, Charlot was spewing words between his teeth. "Damn old stupid arse! Stupid enough not to have found the place." The Italian nervously ran his hand over his freshly shaved chin. Nothing good could come out of this talk. They were already late. It was starting wrong, it would end wrong.

Lebeuf, however, was keeping his cool. After all, Stevens was just a man like anybody else. There was no harm in talking to him, even if Riley and Durand had done everything they could to prevent the interview. The stories of retaliatory dismissals that he had heard last night were probably exaggerated. Anyway, he would certainly find out.

"If the old man doesn't show up in five minutes," he said, "we'll go in without him. It won't make much difference in any case."

"Anyway, I don't like this thing at all. I'm givin' it to yuh straight. I don't like it. It's gonna turn sour."

"What difference can it make?" continued Lebeuf. "Old Breton can hardly talk."

"Stupid old arsehole! Yuh'd need to put a leash'round his neck and . . ." His voice suddenly stopped. Bleary-eyed

Pop Breton, looking confused in his tight-waisted suit —
possibly First-World-War vintage — his neck yoked in a
celluloid collar, appeared at the door of the anteroom. He
gazed blankly about and did not seem to recognize his two
companions.

"This the transport company?" he asked in a deafening
voice that caused the secretary to raise her head. "This the
transport company?"

He turned and looked at his partners once more and
it was only then that he recognized them. His placid,
old Indian face relaxed. He moved to Charlot and extended his hand as if he was about to offer him his con-
dolences.

"What have yuh been doin', dammit? Why don't yuh
take off yer hat?"

Charlot looked sideways at the secretary to see if she
had noticed that incongruity. Old Breton was still shaking
the Italian's hand. "Believe it or not," he said, "I left
home at five past eight. Took a streetcar. Hell, 'twasn't
the right one. Ended up in Lachine — Montreal Locomo-
tive. Got on a..."

"You tell us about that later, Pop Breton," interrupted
Lebeuf as he put his hand on the old man's shoulder. "The
important thing is that you made it here."

He then walked over to the secretary's desk and asked
her to announce them.

"What are we going to tell Stevens?" asked the old
man. And his voice reverberated strangely in the ul-
tra-modern office.

Charlot's sour expression invited him to keep quiet.
"Christ, Pop, shut up! Don't say a damn word! That's the
best thing you can do."

As soon as they walked into the office, Mr. Stevens
got up beaming and extending his hand. "How are you,
boys? Glad to see you!"

"Yeah, well how are yuh? Howdy!" sputtered the old man, thrusting his cap in his pocket. Charlot looked daggers at him.

"Please have a seat. I don't often have the opportunity to visit you," Stevens continued in his broken French, "but I am happy to see you. What can I do for you?"

Lebeuf looked at Charlot, who had promised to speak first, but the Italian seemed frozen. Jules made up his mind to go ahead. "We came about Mr. Boulé..."

The director betrayed no surprise. Durand must have briefed him on it. He nodded and pondered for a few moments. "Boys, I'll tell you something. The company has always played fair. We gave Boulé six months' severance pay, and we weren't obliged to do that, understand."

"Bouboule is an old worker. He's about the age of Pop Breton here. He's worked for the company since 1913."

The old man lent an ear as he noticed he was the subject of the conversation. "1913, same year as me. We both got in in the same year."

He looked around him, frightened by what he had just said. He had started the same year, that was true, but he had never hit a supervisor on the head with a broom.

"He's an old man who isn't all there," continued Lebeuf.

"Yes, I know," replied Stevens. "He's an old man who spends his time talking against the company."

Charlot shifted sideways in his chair. *That's it* he thought. *I told them.* Stevens knew everything, absolutely everything. He also knew that Charlot, too, had talked against the company and that he had encouraged Bouboule's revolutionary statements.

"You're Lebeuf, aren't you?" inquired Stevens, turning to Jules.

"Yes."

"You're a student?"

"Yes."

"Yes, I know . . ."

Mr. Stevens took a few steps across the office, biting his lips. Suddenly, he turned to Jules. "Can I speak to you alone for a few minutes?"

Charlot got up, followed by Pop Breton.

"Is it already over?" asked the old man. "Is Bouboule gonna..."

"Go on, go on," said Charlot, pushing him toward the door. "I'll tell you once we're out."

It was quite clear that Lebeuf was going to lose his job. But at least he, Charlot, had pulled out of it. Now it was a matter of playing it cool, watching what you said. There were stool pigeons in the group.

When the two sweepers had gone out, Mr. Stevens sat back in his swivel chair and laid both hands flat on the top of his desk. "Listen, Lebeuf. You're an intelligent man. You've worked at the Hochelaga Shops for more than a year, right? Good! Tell me, man to man, what's wrong at Hochelaga Shops? Please tell me. Boulé, Bill, Marceau, Charlot, et cetera. I hear those names almost every day. From the other shops, almost nothing ever. Tell me what's really the matter?"

Lebeuf wavered for a few seconds. "The thing is," he said finally, "the men don't like Mr. Lévêque."

"They don't say the work is too hard?"

"No... well, they say so, all right, but it's not true. They don't think it is, anyway. Salary is another question. Eighty cents an hour for married men, with kids, you can appreciate what it amounts to."

Stevens's forefinger crept slowly to his mouth as he looked at Lebeuf. "Lévêque is a good employee," he said, "conscientious, reliable. But he lacks psychology."

"The men don't like him," repeated Lebeuf.

"And you?"

140

"Me? I don't like him either."

"No, I meant, do the men like you?"

Jules shrugged. "I'm doing okay. I do my job and..."

"That's not true."

"I beg your pardon?"

"I say, it's not true. The men like you, they listen to you, and they respect you."

Lebeuf made a gesture indicating that he didn't bother with such things.

"Don't say no. I thought about your case when my secretary told me you were coming. If you got that job a year ago, you know, I'm responsible for that. Durand didn't want it. But I told him, 'Listen, Durand, French-Canadian students don't usually work. And they get fewer scholarships than English-Canadian students. Here's one that wants to work, let's try him.' "

"I'm much obliged," said Lebeuf, surprised.

"Don't thank me. You're doing a good job. The company is happy to have you." The boss paused. "To make a long story short, here's what I have to propose. I give you Lévêque's job, same salary, $75.00 a week; I take back Boulé after a three-month suspension and..."

Jules shook his head. No, he did not want that. He refused to go to the other side of the fence and become a foreman. He was part of the sweepers' group. They had been at it together for the last eighteen months. Maybe his mates trusted him. He would not betray them.

"Wait," said Stevens. "That's not all. You say that the salaries are too low. Good. I don't deny it. So, I'll remove two men from the Hochelaga Shops. Three are retiring in Saint Denis and in Mount Royal this year. I'll send Lévêque to Villeray, and I'll give a ten-cent an hour raise, across the board. What do you say?"

Mr. Stevens had talked fast. He must have thought his proposition over for a long time before the sweepers' arrival. Seeing that Lebeuf remained silent, he added, "I'm not asking you to decide right away. Take your time. Think it over. A week, two weeks. Not more though. And... I shouldn't tell you, but let me add this — I've got something else coming for you later."

The boss got up and extended his hand. "Think it over. Good-bye and good luck."

Lebeuf took a step toward the door, then changed his mind. He wanted to get something off his chest. "If I don't accept," he said, "what about Bouboule? What's..."

"It's all or nothing at all." The tone in his voice invited no reply. "Take it or leave it. We make the changes I told you, or we remain as before." Mr. Stevens stretched his arms, indicating he really could not be counted on for more.

Jules nodded that he understood and left without saying any more.

Charlot and Pop Breton were waiting down on the sidewalk, and they ran toward him as soon as he showed up.

"So, what did Stevens tell you?"

Lebeuf shrugged his shoulders. "I'll tell you some other time."

Charlot opened his mouth as if to ask a question also, but he remained silent. *Just as I'd thought, he got the sack. It was too bad because basically he was a good guy after all. It's not my fault* he continued reflecting to himself. *I warned him.*

"Well, we'll see you around then," Charlot said finally as he walked away with old Breton.

VI

Lebeuf felt depressed. *Why? There was no reason at all.* Stevens had offered him a position he did not want. The student had refused, or almost refused. Anyway, he would refuse if any new propositions were made to him. Nothing had changed. Life would go on as before. There was no cause for depression.

Standing in front of the Metropolitan Transport Building, Jules hesitated. Should he go back to his room right away? Go for a drink somewhere? Try to meet with Weston? Go over to the library? Bypassers were hurrying down Place d'Armes to catch streetcars at the terminus. Continuously the cars were trundling out of the station with a clanging roar, ringing their loud bells as they turned on to Craig Street. Jules followed the crowd. He slowly walked across the tracks and went into the terminus. The same problem was on his mind. It was not true that nothing had changed. Life could not go on exactly as before. First of all, there was Bouboule, who was responsible for the whole thing. Should he be left to suffer his fate? Should they dissociate themselves from him after having made a move on his behalf? The poor old man must be in despair. What would he do now at the age of sixty-three, with no pension, no job, no means? *I'll have to go and see him* thought Jules. But that was not all. Stevens' proposition concerned Lebeuf himself, too. Whether he refused or not, his life would be changed as a result of it. This was a time for soul-searching. *What am I really?* A student to be sure. He took courses at the university. But he was not a student like the rest. He was much older than average to begin with. He had lived, worked. Unlike the majority, he had not been pushed into university by his family or social status. He studied because he wanted to, because of a dream nurtured for years. Weston was the only other student he knew to be in such a situation...

Lebeuf stopped to have a look around. Passengers were running across the long waiting room, surrounded by newsstands, small shoe-repair, florist and tobacco shops. Some people looking concerned went from one bystander to the next asking for directions. On the platform, an inspector, dressed in a gold-striped uniform, was busy noting down the streetcars' arrival times. A few rural types, easily recognized by their tanned faces and badly fitting clothes, stood in awe of the hustle and bustle.

"Well, hi there, Lebeuf! You don't recognize anybody anymore?"

It was a sweeper Lebeuf had known at Hochelaga. He used to pick up butts and papers with a long-handled pole.

"Hi," replied Lebeuf as he went on walking.

He did not feel like chatting. He took out his pipe and started smoking. *I am a sweeper, too, just like that guy*. At least he had been, up to now. All his studies, his intellectual pretensions, were they not all a put-on, something artificial, a way of forgetting, of escaping? From what, from whom? Lebeuf had no special anguish from which to escape. *I'm normal, healthy and pretty hardy*. It was hard to imagine a fellow more uninvolved, more free... Of course, there was Marguerite, who hung on to him. But that was not the point. Her hold was only skin-deep, only a habit. *Nothing essential*.

Lebeuf suddenly found himself engulfed by a sea of

people wanting to catch a streetcar. A woman lost her hat. Jules picked it up for her. The lady had great blue eyes, round cheeks, a turned-up nose. She mumbled her thanks and went rushing on. Lebeuf leaned against the smokeshop window. *Am I tied to my province? To French Canadians? To all this, in fact?* He was aware of the hubbub in the terminus, one of the vital spots in Montreal, a focal point of activity. *Do I feel "happy" and "at home" here?* At times during discussions with Weston, Jules would grow heated, would show enthusiasm or disgust, sincere but doubtless exaggerated. Had he felt especially nostalgic during his three years in Boston? Anything different from any young man who had just left his hometown to be plunged into a new milieu with a different language and different attitudes? Yet Jules had come back to Canada. Very probably he would never leave the country again... But what had he been doing since his return? Was he helping his compatriots? Had he joined a political movement? Was he involved in social action groups? Was he even thinking of settling down with a wife and kids? No, always no. Fundamentally, all those things did not interest him. At least not directly, not in themselves. He would have liked to express them, sure enough, to give them life, and shape, but they did not captivate him in themselves. The big man shrugged. *I am an imbecile, a dreamer.* His only claim to distinction was to be both a sweeper and a student at the same time. Nothing more. And even that he owed to external circumstances. He had showed up at the Transport Company and had been hired — thanks to an English official who thought that Québécois students did not have enough scholarships. *A nightclub Socrates.* Lebeuf bent over to empty his pipe and suddenly the problem which had triggered off that chain of thought came back to mind — Bouboule, the position of foreman... He decided to go

145

back to his room. He would let Marguerite in on it, would tell her about his intention to refuse. He was asking for a terrible argument. So what? It was better than not talking to anybody about it. *I'll see Weston later on.*

There was a shifting in the midst of the crowd and Lebeuf found himself pushed violently into a streetcar. No sooner were they in than people rushed to the empty seats with wild determination. The conductor barked, in both languages, instructions that no one paid attention to, then the old car screeched and lurched on. Lebeuf remained standing at the back.

"Hi there," he said, greeting the conductor as soon as the latter raised his head from his work.

"Hey there, how are you? Still at Hochelaga?"

"Yeah."

"You know what the sons o'bitches wanna do?" Jules shook his head.

"They wanna put one-man cars on this line! Makes no bloody sense. Between you and me it makes no goddamn sense."

Lebeuf nodded approvingly.

The conductor went on talking. He was a sad-looking man in his fifties with a bushy moustache. "But there's gonna be a lot o' shit. Bang, bang." His right fist pounded into his left palm. "Bang. Bang. We're waiting for them. They're askin' fer it."

The doors banged open, which brought an end to the confidential talk.

"Des deux côtés, bote sides; *avancez en avant,* dere's room; *attention aux portes,* mine the door!"

As soon as he was through with his job of jamming a throng of passengers farther toward the front, he turned to Lebeuf once again. "They don't know what they're letting themselves in for. Bang! Bang! Just wait and see. We weren't born yesterday. On a one-man car, my boy, a man

146

has to work like two men. Figure it out for yerself. Here there's two of us. The guy on the one-man car is all by himself. Figure it out for yerself. That's twice the work-load.'' The man seemed proud of his reasoning. ''Up front my friend,'' he said to a passenger who was blocking his sight of Lebeuf. ''There's no way out of it,'' he continued quickly. ''Whichever way yuh look at it. Twice the workload. And yuh know what they're givin' on top o' that? Ten cents! Can you imagine? Ten cents ain't twice a buck ten; that's easy to see!''

The doors folded open once more with a loud crack. *Laissez débarquer*. Let'm get off. Take your time. Dere's lots o' room. Hurry up. *Dépêchez-vous; si vous restez su'la marche on part pas;* mine de door.'' The doors snapped shut again with a noise of breaking dishes, slapping the backsides of the last passengers.

The conductor called Lebeuf with a motion of the hand. He was not through talking yet. ''As I was sayin', a man on the one-man car, he has the job of two. There's no way around it. On the other hand, ten cents is ten cents, and a buck ten is a buck ten. It's not hard to figure out. Right?''

''You're right,'' replied Lebeuf.

''But, just wait a minute! They don't know what they're lettin' themselves in for. Heads are gonna roll. We're dry behind the ears, if they're not. Just wait and see...''

A new swarm of passengers cut the thread of his reasoning. But this time people piled against one another so much that they blocked his sight of Lebeuf completely. Impossible to push them frontward. Overwhelmed, the conductor began to punch out transfers. Jules elbowed his way out a few stops later.

Once he was out on the sidewalk, he asked himself once more if he should go home and tell Margot about it. But he kept coming up with the same answer. He had to tell someone, even if it was only to hear himself articulate the reason for refusing. It would give weight to his arguments. As far as Margot's arguments were concerned, he already knew what they would be, and he was irritated in anticipation. *We definitely have to break up once and for all.* Marguerite was holding him back, turning him into a bourgeois. And yet, when it had begun, he had imagined that the set-up would bring him peace of mind and the opportunity to work and be productive!

VII

As soon as he reached the landing, the door opened and Marguerite appeared, smiling. She was wearing a gray jersey dress, which hugged her breasts, and a little red apron with a heart-shaped pocket. Lebeuf looked at her with mixed feelings of affection and regret. Was he really going to leave her soon? Was the Bouboule affair going to precipitate the break? Jules kissed Margot with more passion than he intended, then he went and sat down by the window.

"Looks like you got all dressed up eh, Jules. I saw your suit wasn't in the closet when I came back. What's happening?"

"Nothing much," replied Lebeuf.

She looked at him incredulously for a while as she began to set the plates on the folding table. "Nothing much? Don't come and tell me that, Jules Lebeuf. You're the one who hates dressing up. Now you're gonna tell me you got all dressed up for nothing?"

"I saw Stevens this morning."

Margot pouted disapprovingly. "Stevens? Is he your boss?" Once more Jules had had to risk his neck for his fellow sweepers.

"Yeah, he's the big chief," answered Lebeuf.

Margot momentarily interrupted her questioning as she became engrossed in trimming her steak, a nice slice of

149

meat which she had bought at the Saint Jacques Market. "Then why did you see him?" she asked as the operation came to an end.

"A delegation. We had something to request on behalf of one of the boys."

Margot sighed as she dropped a big dollop of butter in the pan. Then she added the steak, and they could hear it sizzling. "So, did it work out all right?"

Lebeuf waited for the sizzling to stop. "Well, just imagine, he offered me a foreman's job, seventy-five smackaroos a week."

"Seventy-five bucks a week! Seventy-five bucks? We're gonna be rich, Jules!" She rushed over and gave him a clinging kiss. "A foreman! Jules is gonna be a foreman! Can't wait to see the girls'faces at the restaurant when I tell 'em about that. Foreman! Just think of that!" The steak threatened to burn. She rushed back to shut off the gas.

"You don't think I accepted, do you?" asked Lebeuf as he sat down at the table.

Margot was startled. "Have you lost your marbles, Jules Lebeuf? Seventy-five bucks a week and a foreman's job to boot!"

Lebeuf had a first bite of his steak; the meat melted in his mouth. "You think I'm a fink or something."

Margot's mind was off the food now. "A fink? I don't see what that has to do with it. Seventy-five dollars a week! You and your finks! What's a fink in the first place?"

"A fink's always on the boys' backs, licks the bosses' boots. Not my bag, you should know that," answered Lebeuf.

Margot pursed her lips. So that is what it was! She should have known. There was no love lost between bosses and herself either. But you needed bosses around.

Otherwise nothing could work. You had to do your best to become a boss yourself, that was all. For a while now, Marguerite had had the ambition of becoming head waitress at the Super. The girl who was head waitress now was soon going to get married, making Margot the second oldest in the place. It was bound to come before too long. Her salary, too, would almost double as a result of the promotion. And after a few years' saving, what could stop her from having her own restaurant, or even a motel with a dining room somewhere on the highway near the American border? Jules could tend the cabins while she managed the restaurant. If they lived in the country, then Jules would not have all kinds of guys to hang around with in nightclubs. His literary mania, his earth-shattering theories would gradually disappear. He would marry her, to be sure. That would be happiness.

Her thoughts suddenly returned to the current discussion. The dreamy glitter disappeared from her eyes. She heaved a sigh. No use getting carried away; she had to proceed carefully. Jules had crazy ideas on occasion. At such times it was better not to attack him too violently, but to wait, to change tactics. After a pause, Margot went on eating. Then she got up to pour the coffee. Jules was observing her from the corner of his eye.

Once she had wolfed down her meat, Margot sat with a steaming cup of coffee between her hands and said calmly, "Bosses have always been around and they'll always be around. Neither you nor I is gonna change a thing 'bout it. If not you, somebody else's gonna be the foreman. And anyway, you're always best on the right side of the fence."

Lebeuf gritted his teeth. Here was one of the arguments he had come up with for himself on his way back from the head office. Margot had spoken calmly. He was left with no reason to get mad. He had not even mentioned

151

Bouboule. *I must see Weston no later than tonight. Before going to work.* He had been crazy to mention the business to Margot.

VIII

The schoolgirls came out of the convent all chatter and giggles. The clusters of friends, which the classroom's alphabetical order had momentarily broken up, were being formed again. By force of habit, Gisèle walked toward Jeanne and Pauline. The first girl was the daughter of a doctor, the second of an accountant. But class distinctions in no way impaired the relationships between the girls so long as they were in the confines of the school. However, neither Jeanne nor Pauline would visit Gisèle at home; she had gone to their homes two or three times, but then had stopped as a matter of pride. Their smiling evasion of her oft-repeated invitations had deeply humiliated Gisèle. She was part of the group but a little like a poor cousin. Although she understood her friends' attitude, she had never quite forgiven them.

But such reflections did not weigh too heavily on her at the moment. She was smiling happily as she absent-mindedly answered their question. "Nothing wrong," she repeated. "I just don't feel like talking, that's all."

Her two friends were not fooled by that. There must be something. First her day away from school, then her mysterious attitude the next day. And today her incredible absentmindedness, for which she had twice been punished by having to stand in front of the class.

"It's your business, if you don't want to talk, my dear," said Pauline sharply, "but we're not blind."

Gisèle did not answer. They would find out later about

it. For the moment she did not want to divulge her secret. Augustin Sillery! What a harmonious, distinguished, aristocratic name! He had been on her mind for the last two days. At last she had met a young man who pleased her, who met her ideal. Such politeness, such refined manners. The elegance of a nobleman. And such gentleness too. He had not even attempted to take her hand in the taxi. If he had tried, she certainly would have let him... Had he found her too young, too much of a child? That thought cast a shadow over the jubilation for a while...To think that Lebeuf was the one who had occupied her thoughts for a week! She had not even known that Augustin existed forty-eight hours ago. Maybe Jules Lebeuf was intelligent, as her father claimed, educated also, since he went to university with Augustin, but he was common. He had the manners and almost the language of a sweeper. Whereas with Augustin it was even impossible to understand what he was saying at times. *Was I clumsy with him? No, I don't think so.* Augustin's attentive, flattering way had persisted. Gisèle had been "reserved"; she had been on her guard, oh yes. She had not said much. She was almost sure of it. But it was not necessary to talk a lot with him — he made her feel that she was interesting. He understood and guessed so well. And he made conversation with such ease, with such command of the language and in an accent so melodious it would have been wrong to interrupt him.

The three schoolgirls had reached the corner of Pius IX and Saint Catherine Streets. Jeanne and Pauline were conversing animatedly.

Gisèle suddenly came out of her daydreaming. "Excuse me. I've got to make a phone call."

"You want us to wait for you here?"

"No, don't bother. It might take a while."

With a bound, Gisèle entered the drug store. She was

154

going to call Augustin. She had come to that decision during the afternoon while serving her punishment in front of the class. The move would not be out of order. All she wanted to do was thank him. She had not sufficiently expressed her gratefulness before leaving him two days ago. The young girl entered the booth and, with a shaking hand, inserted the coin in the slot. She had looked up the number that morning and knew it by heart. Augustin would surely be at home; It was four-twenty. Gisèle felt her left palm grow increasingly clammy against the black receiver. *How crazy can you get! It's only a business call to thank him.*

After his painful conversation with Mrs. Sillery, Augustin had slept till nine o'clock and then gone to the university.

As soon as Sillery had showed up in the corridor, Langevin had walked up to him with his hand extended, blushing slightly. "Sorry, old man, about that episode at the Tigre. Absolutely impossible to get away. A cousin of mine from the country... you know what it's like. When I phoned the club, you were already gone."

Still keeping Langevin's hand in his, Sillery appeared to be racking his memory. "The Tigre?" His face suddenly brightened. "Oh, that! Not important, come on, old man! I stayed there only for a few minutes. I knew it was nothing definite, and I also had a friend to meet at La Bougrine."

He abruptly let go of the young student's hand. Langevin appeared disappointed. After a few trifling remarks, he asked Sillery if he had anything planned for that night.

"Tonight? Sorry, old man," replied Sillery in his falsetto voice. "A boring date, but impossible to get out of it. One of those sticky chicks, the type they don't make anymore."

155

"Tomorrow night maybe?" The young man glanced at Sillery with quasi-supplication in his eyes.

'Tomorrow night?" Augustin snapped his fingers. "What a bother! We're really out of luck. Busy then too. But we'll meet again next week."

Chest out, head high, Sillery made a limp gesture of the hand and walked toward a group of students who had just come in.

When the phone rang, Mrs. Sillery was lying eyes closed, on a pile of pillows listening to *Après-midi d'un Faune*. The heavy, syncopated music, evocative of the forest, had a way of calming her nerves. Today, despite her latest attack, she felt happier than she had in a long while. Augustin had walked in from his lecture like a proper student around two o'clock. At the moment he was no doubt sleeping in his room. Mrs. Sillery regretfully turned off the massive, mahogany record player at the head of her bed and picked up the phone.

"Hello!"

"Hello!" The voice at the other end of the line was young, crystal clear, and betrayed a certain confusion. "Could I speak to Augustin, please?"

That's her thought Mrs. Sillery *it's Gisèle*. She was burning to ask her a few questions, to chat a little. But it would have been indiscreet. "One moment, I'll go and check."

It would have been simple enough to press a button to ring Augustin's room, but she preferred calling the maid. Why wake him up brutally if he was resting?

The three knocks on his door startled Augustin in his bed. "What is it?"

156

"You're wanted on the phone, Mr. Augustin."

He sat on the edge of his bed, rubbing his eyes. "What nut is it who could...?" he muttered. "At four o'clock in the afternoon!" Didn't they know that was his rest period?

"Hello!"

"Hello! Augustin?" The voice was thin, a trickle of water. "It's me, Gisèle, Gisèle Lafrenière..."

Augustin winced with annoyance. *Is that girl going to run after me now?*

"Gisèle! What a pleasure to hear your voice!"

"I'm not disturbing you?"

"But not in the least! I just came in. I was thinking about you." His voice rang false. *Lebeuf is going to pay for this.* There was a giggle at the other end of the line.

"I... I simply wanted to thank you once again for..."

"Oh, well now, Gisèle, it was the least I could do. And it won me the immense privilege of making your acquaintance."

What was this young schoolgirl's relationship to Lebeuf? His mistress? No, out of the question. Then why was he protective toward her? A silence grew. A smile appeared on Sillery's lips. "I hope I'll have the pleasure of seeing you again, Gisèle," he continued with honeyed words.

Obviously, she was enthralled. She must have been swooning at the other end of the line. "Would tonight suit you?"

Augustin would have time to call up Lebeuf and Weston and urgently invite them to some dive in the lowertown district — naturally without letting them know whom he would be escorting. Sillery was anxious to see the expression on Lebeuf's face when he saw Gisèle.

"I could fetch you at your place around nine o'clock maybe?"

'No, not at my place!'

That's right, he thought. *Tight-arsed parents on top of that!* She had not let him walk her back to her door the day before yesterday. *Getting better all the time!* The whole thing was turning out exquisitely. "Where then? Quick, let me know. Don't keep me languishing, wicked girl..."

The same giggle was heard at the other end of the line. *I've got her.*

"The same place maybe. Corner of Adam and Pius IX."

"Very well! I'll be there at nine o'clock sharp."

No sooner had Sillery hung up than he started pacing his room, rubbing his hands. To think that he had had nothing to do after refusing Langevin's invitation... At one point, he was tempted to ring up the young student. He would have liked Langevin to see him when he was with Gisèle. Because she was really pretty, a little doll. Then he changed his mind. *Too soon.* He had to be satisfied with the presence of Lebeuf and Weston.

Augustin lay down again and took up his Pascal. Now was the time for him to devote himself to intellectual matters.

IX

Weston had not seen Lebeuf for two days. Lectures, the library and his own room; for the last forty-eight hours, he had led the life of a model student, as he had during the first days of his stay in Montreal. He had thought of phoning Jules a couple of times, but had been reluctant to do so. *If he wants to see me* he thought *he knows where to find me. All he has to do is come to the lectures...* Actually, the American had not been unhappy with the two-day reprieve.

But the night of the second day, an incident had occurred. As he was coming into the house, around eight o'clock, Thérèse had walked out of the kitchen, as if by chance. She had declared, "Americans are making themselves scarce... no doubt because the tourist season is over."

Ken had agreed to have tea with her in the kitchen. Deep down, he did not have a clear conscience, and he reproached himself for neglecting her. Thérèse had done him precious favors. Thanks to her, he had been able to speak decent French as early as the end of his first month in Montreal. And in addition, she did his laundry free...

When Thérèse had almost absent-mindedly started to talk about the restaurants and cabarets of the city, Weston had made a benevolent move. He had asked her if, as they had agreed a few days earlier, she still wanted to go with him to La Bougrine that very evening. Thérèse had objected for a while, then had finally agreed. She was enchanted.

But since Mrs. Beauchamp went to bed at nine-thirty and Thérèse did not want her mother to suspect her "escapade," they planned to leave at ten o'clock.

Meanwhile, Weston had locked himself in his room to "work on his thesis." No sooner had he sat down than Lebeuf had phoned to tell him that he, too, was going to La Bougrine, around ten-thirty, before work. A run of bad luck. How would he get out of it? Thérèse would gripe a little because she despised Lebeuf. She found him rough and unmannerly. Weston hung up with a sigh and returned to his thesis.

He opened *Au pied de la pente douce* and started to read. At the beginning of his session at the university, "working on his thesis" meant something precise — putting down on paper his impressions of French Canadians. He had covered some forty pages in that way. Then little by little, as "discoveries" became rarer, "working on his thesis" had taken on an increasingly vague meaning. First, confident as he was working on the research phase, he had amassed documentation. He had piled up statistics — population, life span, commerce, industry, imports, exports, professions, salaries, government, natural resources, etc. Then he had delved into the historical aspect, had forced himself to read the entire works of Garneau and had leafed through Chapais, Groulx and two books by Frégault. A good fifty pages between the covers of a second copybook bore witness to his hard work. He could have also read works on ethnography, Canadian or foreign, specifically dealing with "his subject." But he refused to do it. Or at least he preferred to wait till his own work had taken shape.

But that was it — it was *not* taking shape. How could he fit together so many disparate pieces of information?

160

Some of the information dealt with the past, some with the present. A good part came from personal observations; a bit had been gleaned from books, and some of that seemed false. Should he try to refute those points? In other respects, some of the literature's observations appeared fair; what then was the use of repeating them? And a lot of them, although quite interesting, were not "part of the topic," although he did not quite know why, or even exactly what the topic was. For months now he had been floundering through this intellectual fog. Finally he had ended up simply reading at random, sometimes with delight but most of the time with boredom — French-Canadian novels, collections of poems, magazine articles or even newspapers. He was doing it out of "duty," out of stubbornness, to prove to himself that he would not give up.

Meanwhile, he kept seeing Lebeuf and Sillery. He talked with other students. Perhaps all this was not, as he had thought the other night, a waste of time. Perhaps some unfathomable maturing process was taking place unconsciously within his mind. But it was true that he had also talked with Germans, Frenchmen and Englishmen while he was in Europe without appreciable results.

Sitting at his paper-strewn desk, head in his hands, Lemelin's novel to the left, *Le Devoir* on the right opened to the sports section, Weston reflected upon his thesis. His thesis? Self-mystification probably. Like his dream of becoming a journalist. He would doubtless end up like his two brothers, employed in an agricultural machinery factory where his father was foreman. Ken had worked there for two summers during holidays before the war. Pitiful! Smoke, the din of machines, grease, the ordeal of standing on one spot for eight hours straight in front of a lathe... Yet the following summer he had wanted to take it up again. His father had needed all his paternal authority and influence to send him back to college. Ken had thought he was in love with Jenny, a young working girl and neighbor. She was blond, languid, with a southern drawl. He wanted to marry her. Now she had three kids and was living in a hovel on the outskirts of St. Louis with a drunken husband.

Weston folded back his *Devoir* and stretched his long muscular arms. The strange thing was that he was not unhappy. Not at all. His present life did not displease him. A consequence of the war no doubt. The time spent at the front had turned him into a philosopher. If you feel no pain, are deprived of nothing, you can count yourself lucky, he had often repeated to Lebeuf. And he believed it. When you settled down, got older, had more money, you had more worries and, generally speaking, not such good health. Ken recalled, with almost poetic nostalgia, soldiers from the most miserable backgrounds talking about their childhood and homes. Now they had been discharged and were doubtless telling their friends all about the good times they had had in the army. Probably Weston himself would later become sentimental about his life as a Montreal student during the 1940s. He would recall his discussions with Lebeuf in cafés, Sillery with his inimitable tirades. Thérèse also, the old maid of clumsy but touching affection... Then why not start looking at things from that angle now?

Kenneth took a few steps across his rocm, lit a third cigarette. *I smoke too much.* A recent American novel, which his brother had sent him, lay on his night table. Ken had not opened it. *Not a line of English read in almost four months. Quite a feat.* It seemed as though his thesis was not getting anywhere, but who knew? Some morning he would probably wake up with a clear, precise, dazzling theme in his mind, and he would start writing. Anyway, he was improving his French. There was no doubt about that. Often during conversations he would forget it was not his own language. Half the time at least he thought directly in French. It was hard to imagine an easier way to learn a language than to use it with friends. And of all the friends he had made, Lebeuf was the one with whom he felt most at ease, most close.

Weston stretched again and decided to go back to his thesis. His ramblings never brought him anything new. Pencil in hand, he brought himself back to reading Lemelin's novel, forcing himself to note the linguistic peculiarities in the dialogue.

He had gone through only a few pages when he heard a scratching at his door. Thérèse slipped into his room with the excitement of someone involved in an intrigue. She wore a canary-yellow dress with a huge red flower pinned to the neckline. She had rouged both her lips and cheeks. Weston repressed a smile when he saw her.

"I'm sorry to intrude this way on the meditations of a philosopher, but it won't be time wasted for you, Ken. You'll be able to add to your observations on French Canadian women. What are you reading now?"

Weston showed her the book's dustjacket. Thérèse gave it an absent-minded look, stepping a little further into the room. "I didn't come to check on your reading," she stuttered with a little embarrassed laugh. "I... do you know why I came?"

Weston made a vague gesture with his hand. "No."

"Well, I came for the inspection parade, to see if you approve of my dress."

Arms away from her body, she pivoted around two or three times to give him a chance to judge. Ken bit his lips. The fitted dress — a few years old to be sure — drooped on her haunches in a series of tired-looking pleats. The low neckline accentuated the flatness of the chest, and the scarlet flower jarred with the yellow fabric.

"It's very oomph," commented Weston. "The patrons of La Bougrine will have the shock of their lives."

Thérèse flushed with delight. "What language you use. Oomph! You learned that in the army?"

Kenneth shrugged his ignorance.

"You learn pretty good ones in the army! I'm almost scared of going out alone with you."

Thérèse was scrutinizing him with a happy smile. Weston hesitated. He really felt bad about Lebeuf's call. But he had to let her know. "Don't worry, we won't be alone," he started.

"What do you mean?"

"Lebeuf'll be there also. He's the one that phoned a while ago."

"And of course you agreed!"

"Agreed? I didn't agree to anything. I told him that I... that we were going to La Bougrine. He told me that he would be there too, that's all."

Thérèse pursed her lips. "To each his own. Personally, I can't understand what you find interesting about that fellow."

"You don't know him."

"I know him enough. When he came here, he was dressed like a lumberjack and smelled of alcohol. I had to spend an hour cleaning up the ashes he dropped on the floor."

Weston made a gesture of helplessness. He had not thought that Lebeuf's presence would cause so much resentment.

"Anyway, don't mind me," she added. "I would hate to jeopardize such a beautiful friendship. Still, you could have been considerate enough to let me know."

"But I didn't know myself!"

Thérèse turned sharply. "I'll be waiting for you in the dining room whenever you're ready."

164

She acted as if she was going to slam the door, but she restrained herself in time. Mrs. Beauchamp must not find out what was going on.

Weston shook his head and went back to his reading.

X

A few minutes later, Ken began to feel remorseful. He had proposed the outing to please Thérèse, and now Thérèse was unhappy. *And yet I'm not responsible*. Was it his fault that Lebeuf had phoned? Could he possibly have told him not to show up at La Bougrine, that he did not want to see him? *No, it's not my fault*. Still, he understood Thérèse's reaction. The old maid couldn't stand Lebeuf. She must have dreamt about this evening out for the last three days... Weston opened the closet and slipped his jacket on. *I'll offer to leave right away. This way we'll have some time for a tête-à-tête.*

Staring blankly, hands at her side, Thérèse sat in a rocker in the middle of the living room. In her precious evening gown with the red flower, she looked pathetic.

"I decided to leave earlier," said the American. "This way we'll have some time just by ourselves... If that's all right with you."

"Oh! Well, so far as I'm concerned, anything you want. I'm only a guest." She was still playing offended, but Weston saw that she was happy.

"I though we'd take a taxi to get there faster." His French was: *"J'ai pensé que nous prendrons..."*

"J'ai pensé que..."

"Que?" Weston did not understand right away that Thérèse was correcting his French.

Now she smiled protectively. "Oh yes... *'que.'* "

When he was talking with her, Weston multiplied stupid mistakes. And the certainty that he was going to make mistakes and that she was going to correct him removed all charm from their conversations. Why did he not ask her, at least for tonight, to put the grammar aside? But she would surely find him ungrateful and would feel hurt.

La Bougrine was almost empty. At one side, on a small platform made of logs, the Trio Canayen — violin, guitar, accordion — was scraping out country gigs. The main show would not be on till ten-forty-five.

After pocketing the dollar bill Ken had slipped in his hand, the waiter showed them to a small table close to the stage. To be sure, Thérèse would prefer this to the huge tables, as long as sidewalks, along which most of the customers sat.

The old maid sat opposite Weston; she was bright-eyed and excited, like a young debutante. "But Ken, you've brought me to a veritable lumberjack camp. Deep in the forest, like somebody who's cooking up some evil trick! I'm lucky I know you."

"It's the only cabaret in Montreal that's different."

"It's not at all the way I'd imagined."

Weston smiled. "Naturally."

"A real wolf's lair..."

Ken did not answer. That type of naiveté disarmed him.

"So, you're still decided on going back to St. Louis in June?" asked Thérèse, as she brought her glass to her lips.

"Yes, six weeks from now."

"But your thesis wont't be finished, will it?"

Weston gestured his indifference. "No."

"Our lodgers will be gone this summer. You'd be alone..."

Ken turned a deaf ear. It was the third time that she had

167

fed him that piece of information.

"I bet you're counting the days." The old maid was looking him straight in the eye.

"Oh, well, you know, I'm used to being away," said Weston.

Thérèse took a swallow of her highball, which made her wince. "Yes, of course, here or elsewhere, all the same, isn't it? Europe and all... Montreal must seem rather boring."

"I didn't say that."

Thérèse bent over her purse as if to look for something. She could not find it. "And then, there must be some young American girl over there waiting for you."

"I told you. There used to be a young American girl. She's married now. She has three children and is living in a 'slum,' whatever the word for that is in French.

"'*Taudis*.'"

"*Taudis*."

"Yes, I think I remember now. It wasn't very nice of her."

"Things like that happen." replied Weston.

Thérèse had another go at her drink. "There are probably some you never told me about..."

Ken repressed a gesture of impatience. Why was Thérèse always harping on the same thing? "There's fifty minutes left before the show," he said. "We have time for a few drinks."

Thérèse pursed her lips. "Right. I was forgetting. We're here to drink."

She took her highball and drank it up in one draft. She grimaced.

"You're going a bit fast," said Weston. "You've gotta start slowly and speed up the process later."

"I'm sorry, I haven't had much practice." The tone was cutting.

168

Ken shrugged. "Okay." He, too, emptied his glass. "Waiter, two more. You like that?" he asked Thérèse.

"No, but it doesn't matter."

As soon as the waiter came back, she grasped her glass doggedly. She downed the drink in one shot with an obvious effort, the sinews of the neck flexing under the skin.

She's gonna make herself sick thought the American. *Gonna be pretty shitty if Mrs. Beauchamp notices anything.* But the evening was still young. He would surely have the time to sober her up before then. In turn he swallowed his whiskey in one shot.

"Are we having a good time, Thérèse, or aren't we?" he said to her in English.

"It's stupid. I find it completely stupid! Is this how you spend your nights?"

Weston shrugged mockingly. "Yes, although there's one thing. I drink like a civilized person."

Thérèse broke into a high-pitched and unexpected laugh that made a few drinkers turn around. "That's a good one." A new fit shook her. " 'Like a civilized person!' " She was trying to imitate Ken's accent. But soon her features froze and she muttered between her teeth, "if there's one person in the world I know who is uncivilized... and cruel, it's you, Kenneth Weston."

The American's piercing gaze rested for a while on the old maid, who now sat with her head lowered, her face frozen back into a scowl, playing with the snap on her handbag. *She is unhappy* he thought to himself. A few kind words came to the tip of his tongue, but he held them back. *That would only make things worse.*

"I don't know what you mean," he replied. "You drink too fast."

Thérèse uttered a constrained laugh. "As if it made any difference to you! Unless you find that interesting enough

169

for your thesis on French-Canadian ways.''

Weston smiled and pulled his notebook out of his pocket. ''I hadn't thought about that. Drink, Thérèse, I'm taking notes.''

The old maid's temper suddenly flared. ''You want to see me completely drunk? Is that what you want? Well, then, that's what you'll get!''

Grabbing hold of her glass with both hands, she tilted her head back to empty it faster. ''You see, it's not so hard.''

''Indeed,'' said Weston imitating her performance, ''it's easy.''

He was on the point of ordering a fourth round when Lebeuf's massive shape appeared in the entrance. Weston heaved a sigh of relief and beckoned to him. Making his way through the chairs, the big man walked toward them with his heavy gait. As usual, he was wearing a brown leather jacket and a turtleneck pullover.

''You know Miss Beauchamp?'' asked Weston.

Thérèse merely nodded a cold greeting. Lebeuf looked at her with surprise, then sat down without making any comment. ''Sillery's not here yet?'' he asked.

''Sillery? No. He's supposed to come?''

''Yeah. He gave me a ring a while ago.''

''Oh!''

''Don't worry about it, Ken Weston! Don't bother,'' interrupted Thérèse. ''Just tell me how many people you've invited to come and join us here. That way we can take a larger table right away.''

''What are we drinking?'' asked Jules, without paying any more attention to the woman.

''We're drinking highballs, nothing but highballs, we're not doing anything else,'' Thérèse commented in a shrill voice.

'Well then, double for me,'' ordered Lebeuf.

The cabaret was beginning to fill up. At the next table a bunch of Americans were talking excitedly. Farther down, a group of about ten tourists, shepherded by a guide, were settling down on the roughly hewn benches, exclaiming in English.

"Very typical!"

"I must write Dave about it."

"What's the name of this place, dear? I mustn't forget."

Waiters were fluttering about the tables, wearing their obsequious smiles. Standing near the door, the regulars were waiting for the tourists to sit down so they could sit at the same tables. They walked around looking relaxed and natural as if on the lookout for a better place. Some would sit down next to well-dressed, middle-aged American women, who had the reputation of being easy and generous. Others would look for the company of men with a view to asking them whether they felt like a good time after the show. In that case, they always knew the right spots.

"Yeah, well here's mud in your eye while we can still see each other," said Lebeuf as he raised his glass.

He wanted to clink glasses with Thérèse, but she pretended not to see him. Jules looked at Weston. The American merely raised his eyebrows. *A couple of whiskies and I'll take off* Lebeuf told himself. There was no question of bringing up Bouboule's case with that battle axe around.

He paused for a while, then asked, "How's your thesis coming along?"

Weston did not have the time to answer.

"Perfectly well, let me assure you," said Thérèse in the same shrill voice. "The gentleman is now making observations from life. He has guinea pigs."

"Guinea pigs?"

"She's had too much to drink," said Weston.

"That's exactly it, guinea pigs," continued Thérèse. "I am told that you students from the faculty of letters look for inspiration in joints like this. We're going to see some fine results!"

Lebeuf frowned. His big expressionless eyes stared blankly. "If you're interested in novels à la Delly," he replied, "La Bougrine is not the place. You won't find them here."

"Don't bother," insisted Weston. "She's had too much to drink."

"I don't know what interests you," said Thérèse, "or rather I have a clue. It's probably pornography."

Lebeuf opened his mouth to answer, then shrugged, and downed his drink. "Same thing again." he ordered. *I am certainly not going to start a literary discussion with a constipated bitch like that*. A long silence ensued. The show was about to begin. The waiters worked on the double, red pompoms swinging from the strings of their tuques.

"Good evening, lady and gentlemen!" Sillery's soft voice came as a happy diversion. Nobody had seen him come in. Lebeuf had his back turned to him. "I am immensely sorry to interrupt such an animated conversation..."

Why was Augustin not sitting down? Jules turned around and nearly choked on his drink. Gisèle was there, standing in front of him and giggling. In one leap the big man was on his feet. "What are *you* doing here?" Thérèse and Ken were looking on with interest. "Eh? What are you doing here?"

Gisèle blushed and gave Augustin a worried look. *I should have known* thought Lebeuf. *The disgusting twerp. I should have known that he'd try something like that.* He had rarely felt so exasperated.

172

"You want to know what she's doing here?" replied Augustin in his most suave accent. "You have a tragic lack of imagination, my dear! Come on, reflect on it, make an effort."

Jules kept silent. He felt like smashing that effeminate mug, and the wish tensed his muscles. He was surprised by the intensity of his anger.

"No, but really? Don't you find it's a bit much?" The scene was even more delightful than Sillery had imagined. "She came over to have a few drinks and see the show, did you not, Gisèle?"

Gisèle, cheeks aglow and bright eyed, nodded her approval. Lebeuf's presence upset her somewhat. What would happen if he decided to warn her parents? But she drove away that worry. She felt secure with Augustin. Nothing could affect her.

Sillery was going to add something when a waiter, looking worried, came up to him in a hurry, took his arm and pulled him slightly aside. "Listen, my friend, I don't wanna spoil your fun, but the girl with you looks kind o' young. We can't let minors into this place. I'm really sorry about it. I know you're a good customer and the whole bit, but..."

"She's twenty-two, going on twenty-three soon," replied Sillery with assurance. "I should know: she's my sister."

The waiter looked at him with an air of disbelief. "The cops often drop in for a visit, and if they catch us serving minors, believe you me, the fun's over."

"Don't have to worry about that," answered Sillery, as he slipped a five-dollar bill into the waiter's hand. "My father is a member of the provincial parliament. Lajeunesse, you must've heard his name?"

The waiter had a look at his boss joking with a group of tourists. The situation was delicate. "Listen then" he said

173

as he pocketed the bill. "I'm gonna do yuh a favor. I'll sit you in that corner over there. The curtain will hide you a bit. You can sit the girl closer to the wall. I think that should work out."

"Fine."

Sillery felt relieved. If Gisèle had not been let in, the evening would have been down the drain. He came back to the table. The young woman had not moved. Looking worried, she stood behing Lebeuf's chair as he seemed to have forgotten her presence.

Augustin walked over full of self-assurance. "Well, imagine, gentlemen. He wanted me to sing... a little song... like the other night. Do you remember?"

Lebeuf grabbed hold of his arm. Sillery repressed a grimace. "I'm warning you," said Jules, "friend or no friend, if you..."

Augustin felt that things were getting hot. Lebeuf had a murderous look on his face. "No way, my dear... I made that sweet boy understand that such lyrical flight happens only once a century, especially in Canada."

The suave waiter seemed nervous. He wanted to push Lebeuf toward the corner, but the latter freed himself abruptly. Sillery intervened. "Yet, he has offered, in recognition of our past services to put us in a handier corner and to treat us to a first round on the house. Isn't that right, my good man?" he added with a wink.

"Right you are, sir." Long years of service had taught him to lie with aplomb.

Lebeuf followed the others without protesting. Weston offered his arm to Thérèse, who was a trifle unsteady on her feet. As for Sillery, he escorted Gisèle with great histrionic gestures, her silly giggle reverberated objectionably in Jules' ears. *That bugger's gonna pay for this. He won't get away with it.* Rightly or wrongly, he felt responsible for the incident. What would Bill say if he

174

ever found out about his daughter's escapade? Lebeuf was sure that she had not breathed a word to him.

As soon as they were seated at the table, a big vocalist with a huge bust strutted on stage wiggling her backside. "A second Madame Bolduc, the country nightingale of Quebec," the emcee hollered. She wore a ragged peasant dress that left half her left breast exposed and uncovered her enormous, flabby thighs at each step. She began to sing like a clucking brood-hen. The off-color song told how a traveling salesman had showed up at her farm house, while her parents were gone, to sell her underwear. At the end of each stanza, the audience was jumping for joy. The "country nightingale" was making a big hit.

Sillery, noticing Lebeuf's long face, rubbed his hands with pleasure. "A true goddess," he exclaimed. "She could only come from the mating of a nymph and a bull..."

The goddess milked her voice once more:

> *Quand j'eus ôté mon jupon.*
> *Tralala, tralala,*
> *Quand j'eus ôté mon jupon,*
> *Tralala, tralala*
> *Il me d'manda sans façon:*
> *'Auriez-vous pas b'soin, Mamzelle,*
> *Houhouhou, houhouhou,*
> *Auriez-vous pas besoin, Mamzelle,*
> *D'un morceau plus essentiel?'*

As she was singing, the "country nightingale" urged her audience to sing out the "tralala" and "houhouhou" choruses louder.

Jules grew fidgety in his chair. He saw that Gisèle too was beginning to feel ill at ease. A forced smile appeared now and then on her lips. But Sillery patted her hand and gave her an amorous glance.

175

Quand j'eus ôté ma culotte
Tralala, tralala,
Quand j'eus ôté ma culotte
Tralala, tralala,
Il me dit: 'Coute donc, ma crotte'
Houhouhou, houhouhou...

Lebeuf jumped to his feet, grabbed Gisèle by the wrist and pulled her along with determination. "Come on, we're going. This isn't a place for you."

She resisted, holding herself back with all her might. "Let me go, I don't want to leave!"

Augustin got up to help her. "Listen, old man, take it easy. I t's none of your business. I'm the one who escorted her here and it's my intention to..."

Jules slapped him on the shoulder and sent him tumbling back in his chair. "Shut up, or I'll let you have it."

He started toward the exit with quick strides, dragging Gisèle, who was screaming in a shrill voice, "I don't want to leave! Let go of me."

The audience began to boo. It was no longer possible to hear the singer's voice. Some women were shouting indignantly, "What a brute! It's revolting!"

A tall American fellow, who was rather unsteady on his legs, tried to block the way. "Leave her alone, will you! What kind of a rat..."

A jab on the jaw sent him sprawling to the floor. Then, on the manager's signal, three waiters rushed toward the brawler. One of them, a giant with a wrestler's neck, held an empty bottle in his hand. In cases like these, you had to act fast, so you knocked out your man with a well-placed blow, then dragged him out to the rear to let him come to and finally threw him out by the back lane. That way the police did not have time to invervene.

Weston was quick to assess the situation. He had seen all kinds while in the army. That bruiser was capable of breaking Lebeuf's skull. He was up in a wink. Thérèse hung on to his sleeve, trying to stop him. "Ken, I forbid you to go. Let him look after himself!"

Weston slapped her wrist violently against the corner of the table. Thérèse cried out with pain. The American arrived just in time. The bottle was coming down on Jules's skull as he was fighting off three new assailants. Ken took hold of the big waiter from behind. He rammed his knee into his lower back as he blocked his arm and sent him rolling to the floor with a howl of pain. But meanwhile, another waiter, the suave one who had served the so-called house treat, hit Ken on the head with a hard object. Blood came gushing over the left brow. Ken got rid of him with a kick in the stomach, then he no longer grasped clearly what was happening. The floor started to sway under his feet. He saw Lebeuf grab a guy by the feet and mow down half a dozen opponents with a makeshift weapon. He remembered himself having grabbed a young blond fellow by the throat, having carved three bleeding streaks in someone else's face with his nails. Then, finally, a gust of cold air lashed his face. He found himself outside, reeling, his head on fire and throbbing, his left eye swollen. He opened his mouth to catch his breath. A tepid, viscous fluid trickled on his tongue. *Blood* he thought to himself. He then caught sight of Lebeuf standing in the middle of the sidewalk, a barrel stave in hand, ready to dash back into the hall, no doubt to rescue him. A few steps farther, leaning against the wall, Gisèle was sobbing convulsively.

Ken let out a shout. Still watching the entrance, Lebeuf rushed to his friend. "Are you all right, Ken?"

He moved to support Weston as he noticed his friend's face was smeared with blood.

"It's okay. I'm all right."

"Thanks, old man. I'll never forget that. That damn ape with his bottle..."

"Forget it."

"Maybe we'd better go to the hospital. That looks like a pretty bad gash you've got there."

Weston dabbed his face with his handkerchief. "It's okay. I'll go and get Thérèse and go back home." He took a step toward the door.

"But you're crazy! They're gonna knock you out!"

But Weston was deadset. "I'll get her first."

Lebeuf glanced at Gisèle, still there against the wall, her shoulders heaving with sobs. Then, he gripped the club more tightly in his hand and walked closer to the door. Six waiters were guarding the entrance.

'We're not looking for a fight," he said. "My partner here only wants to go in and get his girlfriend who stayed inside."

The waiters looked at each other; Lebeuf's club caused them to think twice. They had no intention of starting the fight again with such a bull of a man.

"Stay here, I'll go in," answered one of the waiters as he disappeared inside.

The big singer had taken up her song again. Once more the "tralalas" and the "houhouhous" of the crowd could be heard. Weston leaned against the door frame. His head was spinning. He felt like vomiting.

"You're sure you're all right?" asked Jules.

"Yeah."

The waiter came back after a few minutes. "She doesn't want to come."

"What? What the hell! It's a trap, Lebeuf, I tell you, it's a goddamn trap," said Weston in English. Weston did not seem too sure of what he meant by that.

The waiters closed ranks.

178

"Do you have any paper?" asked Jules.

A waiter handed his pad and pencil over to him. Weston took hold of it and started scribbling. "Thérèse, will you come out. I want to go home."

The waiter took the piece of paper without saying a word. The howling crowd was heard once more. A minute later the messenger was back with the answer. "I'm not interested. I'm staying. Thérèse."

Weston shrugged, dropped the sheet on the sidewalk. Lebeuf wanted to take him home, but the American refused. "I'll be all right," he said, again in English.

Jules walked up to Gisèle. She stood there motionless, with no expression in her eyes. The sobbing had stopped, but nervous shivers were still running through her body. Her pretty pink dress was torn at the shoulder and long, dark streaks stained her cheeks.

"Come now," said Lebeuf softly, "we'll go back home." She offered no resistance when he walked her over to a cab.

XI

Gisèle was expecting a storm of reproaches. She sat stiffly in her corner of the back seat, getting ready for the attack. *I'm going to stand up to him. I've got to stand up to him, no matter what.* A while back she had cried, but that was because of her nerves. Now she felt calmer. She was ready. Lebeuf was not her father, after all. She owed him nothing...

But Jules remained silent. In the dim light of the street-lamps flashing by on either side of the cab, she saw him repeatedly bring his forefinger up to his swollen cheek and move his jaw with an expression of pain. *He's suffering. Good for him. I'm glad.* The barrel stave rested on the seat next to him. The silence became intolerable.

"I suppose you're going to tell Dad all about it now?" said Gisèle with defiance in her voice.

Lebeuf seemed to come out of a dream. He turned to her. "What? Your father? No, I won't tell him anything, don't worry."

"You can tell him if you want. It doesn't bother me, not a bit, if you want to know!"

Jules remained silent. *She resents me; it's normal.* What was he to her, in fact? Nothing. A stranger, a stranger in whom Gisèle's parents had put their trust and who had come and thwarted the plans of the young scatterbrain. Gisèle was not responsible. Jules was the one responsible. First, he had given in to that ludicrous exam business, then he had introduced her to a character like Sillery. What could he do now? What could he say? He was not even sure he had not yielded to an urge of jealousy when he'd dragged Gisèle out of La Bougrine. *Yet, I don't love her.* No, rather it was a feeling of protection, a fatherly feeling.

The cab was making good time on Sherbrooke Street. The street lights were getting scarcer. Jules could no longer see his companion's face clearly. "Did you get that job with Mr. Sillery the other day?" he asked.

"Yes, I got it."

"You're happy?"

"I haven't decided anything yet." Gisèle felt more relaxed. Lebeuf did not seem to want to reprimand her. "I don't know what my parents are going to think of it," she added.

'Of course, there are a lot of things to consider..."

Gisèle went back on the defensive. "What? What is there to consider?"

"For instance, the idea of pursuing your studies in English. I don't know what Bill's going to think of that."

Is that what he really meant to say? Gisèle did not know what to think any more. Who was Lebeuf? What did he want? That exam, had he really been so reluctant? Anyway, she did not hate him any more. After all, he had fought for her; Augustin had not done anything. After he had fallen back into his chair she had seen no more of him, which was not very chivalrous. If he had gotten up and floored Lebeuf with one smart blow, she would have followed him to the end of the world... In a sudden flash of light the young woman had a quick look at her fellow passenger. Once more he was feeling the contusion on his cheek with his forefinger.

"Your cheek hurts?"

Lebeuf quickly lowered his hand. "Nothing, nothing but a scratch."

Jules was surprised at the joy that simple question had given him. *She's trying to soften me 'cause she's afraid I'll spill the beans.* Yet his joy continued. *That scuffle has shaken me up.*

"Nothing," he repeated. "It'll all be forgotten by tomorrow. And you'll see that things will straighten out for you. I'll talk to Bill."

The cab slowed down to turn onto Pius IX Boulevard. On the left, the flowerbeds of the Botanical Gardens were lined up in the twilight.

"Somewhere around here?" inquired the driver.

"Yes, a little farther down," answered Gisèle. "You can stop on the corner of Adam."

The cabbie drove on for a few blocks, then stopped. Lebeuf got out to let the young woman out. "You want me to walk you all the way to your place?"

"No. I want to see if everybody's in bed. I'll go in by the back."

Lebeuf moved as if to shake her hand. "Well then, good night."

"Good night." Gisèle stood in front of him, facing a street lamp, her dress torn at the shoulder, her cheeks still tear stained. She appeared hesitant: "Well then, thanks a lot," she finally mumbled in an almost inaudible voice.

Jules raised his arm as if to protest, but she was already bolting down toward the alley. He paused there motionless on the corner of the street before getting back into the cab.

XII

After the brawl, Sillery had sneaked out by the back door. Once in the alley that came out on Notre Dame, he stopped. The clucking sounds of the big vocalist still reached him through the wall. *What am I going to do?* His heart was still upsetting him. *Why am I so shaken?* Certainly he had counted on this evening — rather amusing because of Lebeuf's rage — to last till the wee hours of the morning. Then all he would have had to do was to go home and rest, looking forward to his rendezvous with Gaston. Now he found himself alone before midnight... But, after all, it was not the first time. He was used to it. Sillery perfunctorily rubbed his forehead, then drew a circle in the air as if to sweep away something. *That's not the reason...* The old mania of considering nothing but the most superficial aspects of a problem! *It's not the solitude.* It was the recollection of his attitude in the face of Lebeuf's attack, then afterwards during the brawl, that bothered him. *I am nothing but a weak woman. I have the tastes of a woman and the cowardice of a woman.*

He started to go fitfully through his pockets for a cigarette, but to no avail. He must have left them on the table. Applause mixed with whistling reverberated from within. The memory of the brawl became an obsession. *Absurd.* He tried to reason it out. What kind of resistance could he have put up against Lebeuf? The fellow was

183

strong enough to smash him with one clout. It was not cowardice then? He had given in to superior strength, a force of nature. There was nothing to be ashamed of. And the opinion of that silly Gisèle could not affect him. He would not see her again anyway.

Augustin looked through his pockets once more. *Right, I don't have any more cigarettes.* Inside La Bougrine, the Trio Canayen began to play again. Even from outside the strident whine of the violin grated on the eardrum. Augustin started thinking again. The incident had not ended with Lebeuf's being knocked down. The whole place had broken into a fight, and Weston had jumped to help his friend out without hesitation — whereas Sillery had stayed there in his chair, across from that ridiculous old spinster. The student ran his hand across his forehead once more. His hand was clammy. And the throbbing came back. *I've got to do something right away.* His inactivity was becoming insufferable. *Call Langevin?* Yes, that was it. He should call him right away. One more humiliation would not matter. Anyway, he would know how to fix things. He would tell him that he had just dumped the chick after having everything he wanted out of her.

Full of nervous excitement, Sillery started walking toward Craig Street, looking for a drugstore. This time Langevin would not get away from him. Augustin would stop at nothing to get him back. To hell with pride, mincing and frilling of words, to hell with psychological subtleties. A direct, brutal attack. A blitzkrieg. Too bad if the night was to exhaust him, if Gaston was to find him rather flabby on Monday night. He needed a tangible victory immediately.

There happened to be a drugstore on the corner of the street. Augustin rushed to the telephone booth and dialed hurriedly. A distant, exasperating sound rang in his ear.

As long as he's there.

"Hello!"

"Hello! Could I speak to Claude, please?"

"Claude's not here." The tone was cutting, gruff. The father, to be sure. "And let me tell you it's no time to bother people."

Augustin hung up. A wave of sweat swept over his whole body. He glanced at his watch. Only a quarter to twelve. He had at least five hours to go before he could fall asleep. He felt destroyed, annihilated. He leaned his forehead against the dented tin wall of the booth and tried to gather his thoughts. Where to go? The bowling alley? No. He did not want to give Gaston the impression he was running after him. The old Chinaman? No good either. The student felt incapable of sitting at a table for a discussion. All exits were blocked. Augustin felt like screaming and pounding his fist on the booth.

"Are you all right, sir? Can I do anything for you?" The lunch-counter attendant had come over to him.

"No, thank you, everything's all right." Augustin, his face now very pale, lifted his head and made it to the exit, reeling slightly.

"He's sick for sure," said the attendant to his partner.

He looked worried. But the diswasher shrugged. "Don't worry, can't you see he's pissed out of his mind."

XIII

When he got to the car, Lebeuf put down his broom, mop, and pail of disinfectant, then he felt his jaw with his hand and moved his mouth slowly. The cheekbone was not that bad, but every time he tried to open his jaw, even slightly, a sharp pain would shoot through his head to a spot under his left ear. He could not chew anything. After saying goodbye to Gisèle, he had tried to grab a sandwich in a restaurant, but he had had to give it up. He had then run up to his room, gulped down two aspirins and poured steaming soup into his thermos before leaving for work with his lunchpail under his arm.

The clock had read half past twelve as he walked into the shack. There had been no one there. But Bill had punched him in. Everything was all right that way. You could always rely on Bill.

Lebeuf had then picked up his implements and gotten down to work. Memories of the brawl, his ride back in the cab with Gisèle, towards the end especially, floated pleasantly in his mind. Yet nothing extraordinary had happened... Maybe the brawl... *I managed pretty well*. He must have flattened about ten guys. But what had followed was quite trite... A young girl who thanks you because you helped her out!

Although he was working away like an automaton, the job was going well. The day's weather had been fresh, clear and neither too dry — which would have left the inside of the car coated with a thin film of dust — nor too damp — which would have meant clumps of mud on the floor. He had a mere ten trams to go at most when he walked back to the shack for lunch.

The sweepers seemed surprised to see him. They greeted him shyly. Marceau, the big man, even got up to shake hands with him. "How are things, Lebeuf?"

Nobody asked questions about the morning meeting; no comments were made on his black eye either. Nor did they comment when they saw him having soup instead of his customary sandwiches. Conversational topics were neither here nor there and not very animated. *Have they found out what went on in Stevens's office?* wondered Jules. But he rejected that hypothesis. Only Lévêque could have found out, and he surely would not have breathed a word.

The fat cashier stuck his shiny bald head through the wicket. As soon as he noticed Lebeuf's blackened eye, he cried out, "Lebeuf, do you cook on your face now? You got no stove at your place?"

The sweepers did not laugh at that one, and Charlot got up to whisper a few words in the cashier's ear. The cashier nodded understandingly, then slipped back into his cage. Jules was tempted to ask what the mystery was all about. But he hardly felt like a long conversation. The sweepers were not going to question him? Good enough, that would give him more time to think things over. He would not have told them the truth anyway. He wanted to wait, to see Bouboule first.

Going back out to work, Jules took Lafrenière by the arm. "Listen, Bill, would you come with me to Bouboule's on Friday night before our shift. I'd like to see how he's taking it."

"Sure, I'll go for sure. Anything yuh say, Lebeuf. Whenever yuh need me." Bill patted his back in a friendly but shy way.

"At the same time we could talk about the business of your daughter..."

"Sure, sure, of course, Lebeuf, whatever yuh say."

Outside, three sweepers offered to finish his work for him if he did not feel in shape. Jules turned the offer down and walked on with his mop and pail of disinfectant.

Now he was on his last tram. His watch read four-twenty. He had a lot of free time ahead of him.

After dabbing at his cheekbone again, Jules unhooked the trolley's pole and slid the pulley onto the wire. The motor hummed into action. Going back to the front, he pulled a lever under the mudguard; the door opened and he got up into the tram car. The vehicle was American made, one of those the company had recently bought from a Cleveland firm. Jules used it as his reading room. Fortuitously, these cars were equipped with well-upholstered, reversible seats and powerful electric lightbulbs. As the student flicked the switch on, a white light flooded the inside of the car and projected rectangles of brightness along the other streetcars lined up as far as the eye could see inside the huge barn. The entrance door was four hundred feet away. For reading or for sleeping, you always had to set yourself up as far as possible from the entrance and shut the car doors. You also had to set your broom and pail close at hand.

Lebeuf viewed his night reading session as the best period of his day. That was when he was almost sure to be all by himself for between thirty minutes to four hours, when he felt completely sheltered from the outside world, inside this streetcar lost among so many more under the barn's huge and dark roof.

One expert glance and Jules decided this last car did not need sweeping. He merely poured tiny flakes of cleanser near the doors and toward the middle, then spread them lackadaisically with the end of his mop, making sure the car would smell clean. Then, sitting sideways on a seat, his legs resting on the seat ahead and an elbow on the window frame, he opened his book.

Despite the two aspirins, his head ached, and he still felt the dull pain below his left ear. *That guy didn't miss his shot.* He finally started reading. He was going through *Le Père Goriot* once again, from a critical viewpoint for his literature course. The opening description appeared less compelling this time than it had at his first reading. Soon, he raised his head and started daydreaming somewhat sentimentally. Gisèle floated somewhere deep within his mind, but he was not thinking of her precisely. He was thinking about himself , about the position he had been offered, about the Transport Company which he was surely going to quit. Because if he refused the job, he certainly would not hang around very long as a sweeper. And if he accepted it, things would not be the same... With a kind of sadness, Jules looked around him for a long while. He was realizing that if he left, one of the things he would miss most was these periods of reading and reverie at night in an anonymous car, which smelt of dust and creosote, which was too cold in winter, too hot in summer, whose stark ceiling lights tired the eyes. *You always get attached to very simple things like these.* If he left Marguerite, the memory of his untidy room, jammed with pieces of furniture, strewn with papers, littered with laundry piled up in the corners and dirty dishes lying about on the folding table would fill him with nostalgia for weeks, perhaps even for months. He moved his jaw perfunctorily; the pain persisted. *I am at a crossroads* he suddenly mumbled to himself. But the wording seemed too pompous. *I' am falling into the Sillery style.* He sought another expression, could not find any. *Crossroads*; that is what it was. He had to make a choice. Quit the company, look for another job, maybe even leave Montreal... or become a

189

foreman. His gaze rested on the back of the front seat. *Why do I stick to this place?* he asked himself. The sweepers? Of course he had become attached to them; he shared their concerns and their feeling of revolt. Was that the reason? His thoughts went back to his three years in Boston as a textile worker. He had had friends there, too. Friends who, in fact, had accepted him more easily than the sweepers here had. They had even gone on strike together. Lebeuf closed his novel, moved his sore jaw once again. *Why did I come back?* He had a look around him; the streetcar bathed in a milky light, the brighter rectangles consuming the surrounding twilight, the roof top resembling that of an airdrome... All around, invisible and almighty as an ocean, sprawled Montreal with its million and a half inhabitants, Canada's metropolis, his city... *This is where I have my roots.* No doubt this was why he had come back. Because he was part of a small group of French-speaking people lost in a corner of North America... Seen from the outside, his group offered no more interest than did the hundreds of minority groups scattered across the globe. The intellectual climate was far from satisfying. *Nothing unusual about that. The opposite is what would be surprising.* A handful of Frenchmen, peasants for the most part, with no education and deprived of their leaders, had chosen to remain in America after the defeat... They had had to go for first things first — live, till the land, defend their traditions and their language. And they had held on. They had gradually adapted to the new regime; they had tried to make the best of the new situation.

Lebeuf lazily pulled his pipe out of his pocket and began to fill it. The dull pain still lay under his left ear. *What's important is to raise the intellectual level, the rest will follow.* Suddenly his thoughts turned to Gisèle. He saw her shaken with grief and sobs, her face smeared with

190

tears, her dress torn. He saw her again, standing by the taxi, thanking him in a hurry and darting back home. He pushed those images away. *That incident is of no importance. What counts is the fact that she wants to improve herself. I must help her.* Raising the individual's level, wasn't that raising the whole group's level? Lebeuf cracked a match and took a few drags on his pipe. He did not want to get carried away; he was seeking a reasonable course, an objective approach. Gradually, his face relaxed, satisfaction invaded his features. *I'll go and see a psychologist and ask him to give Gisèle a mathematics aptitude test. That way I'll be sure...*

All of a sudden, a loud warning cough reverberated in the car.

"Shit!"

Lebeuf quickly shoved his Balzac into his pocket and started handling his broom. The door was already opening. Lévêque appeared with his shifty little eyes, his high cheekbones and his unctuous mannerisms of a clergyman. He was still wearing a bandage over his left brow.

"Hi there, Lebeuf." He talked slowly, always on the same tone, moving his thick lips like a hen's arse.

Jules went on sweeping indifferently. Lévêque took a few steps inside the tram, rolling his shoulders, and put down his electric lamp on the seat. "This yer last car?"

"Yeah."

Lévêque seemed lost in thought. He puckered his lips as if he had just swallowed lemon juice. "Good job yuh got there, ain't it?"

"No complaints." What was he getting at? He never chatted familiarly with his men. He preferred keeping his distance.

"I know," Lévêque replied sententiously. "I know all about it. I did it for eleven years. In the worst of the Depression."

That piece of information called for no reply. Jules went on sweeping. It was easy for him to see that his zeal annoyed the foreman, who had taken care to forewarn him of his arrival. "Nobody bothers yuh," continued Lévêque. "Yuh go about yer business. How yuh do it, fast or slow, that's yer own business, ain't it? Not a word said, nothing at all, ain't that right?"

Lebeuf nodded. The foreman had picked up the lamp, which he was now rocking at the end of his arm, as if he were giving a signal. He puckered his lips again. "But a fellow gets fed up in the long run, right? A guy who's got something up there, I mean. Yuh know, somebody educated like yuh. It's all right to go along doing yer business, not to be bothered. It's all right for some. They wouldn't ask for more..."

He got wind of my interview with Stevens thought Lebeuf. *Wonder if he knows everything; that I told the boss the men hated him?* Lebeuf let go of his broom. "I don't mind other people's business," he said. "I mind my own."

Lévêque immediately went on with more animation. "That's what some say. 'Mind yer own business, mind yer own business,' but really it's not always that nice and simple. There's many ways of minding yer own business. Some are better, some are worse, right?" His little porcine eyes were eager for an answer.

"No complaints," said Lebeuf.

"No complaints, for sure; that's for sure. I know when I meet the boss sometimes, I sort of tell him, 'Lebeuf is a fellow that never complains, that's for sure.' But sometimes, no matter if yuh complain or not, yuh can still say — and there's nothing wrong with that — still say, 'I'm not complaining a bit, but if I was doing better, I'd complain a lot less,' right?"

"I don't know about what others say," said Lebeuf.

"So far as I'm concerned, I'm not complaining."

Placidly leaning against his broom he was studying Lévêque. The beast was even sneakier than they said he was. Those who had known him before as a sweeper claimed he could repeat the same thing, word for word, ten times in a row in a monotone. Perhaps that was what gave him his strength.

"Ye're not complaining. I know. I didn't say yuh were complaining. But we're just talking for the sake of talking. You're not gonna come and tell me yuh've got it in yer mind to sweep car floors until the good Lord comes to get yuh, right?"

Jules shrugged.

"Don't say that, Lebeuf, now, I don't believe yuh. Don't say that, now." Lévêque wiggled his hen's hole of a mouth to show that he was concentrating. He was getting ready to drop the bombshell. "Here's what yuh say, yuh tell yerself, "I'm single, not married.' That's for sure and certain, I know. I had that job for eleven years, in the worst of the Depression. But don't tell me, Lebeuf, don't come and say that to me. There comes a time when a man thinks that he's single, not married, but things aren't always gonna stay that way..."

One eyebrow raised, the foreman was eyeing Lebeuf to see what effect his words were having. "Right?"

"Could be."

Lévêque put down his lamp and stretched his arm in the way of a preacher. "Don't add a word, not one more word. What I just said makes good sense, right? Yuh'll let me know in a few year's time."

He picked up his lamp and moved back toward the door. He had nothing to add. "See yuh," he said as he went out.

"See you" answered Lebeuf, who waited for him to be far enough away before going back to his seat.

XIV

"What *is* this?"

Lebeuf raised his head, seemingly annoyed. He was going over Gisèle's results on her last test. She had received 137. She came out among the top five percent in her aptitude for mathematics. And that was on a test for adults.

"What *is* this?"

Lebeuf turned and looked at Margot. She was holding a pink cotton glove between thumb and forefinger.

"You can see as well as I do," said Lebeuf, "that it's a glove."

"Yuh think I'm crazy or somethin'. Just as if I couldn't tell a glove when I see one! I want yuh to tell me where it comes from."

Jules slipped the test back in his pocket and hesitated for a while. Standing in the middle of the room, Margot was swinging the glove at the tip of her fingers.

"Just a glove Gisèle forgot," said Lebeuf.

Marguerite dropped the glove. "I didn't want to believe it, but I can see it's true!" She mumbled as if to herself.·

"What do you mean?"

"I know what I know."

She turned her back to him and started to stack dishes in the sink. Jules came and stood beside her. "I asked you what you meant by that."

Margot shrugged and turned on the tap. "Why are yuh asking me that? Yuh know as well as I do."

Jules abruptly turned the tap off. "Explain yourself."

" 'Explain yourself?' Ye're the one who should 'explain yourself.' Some little girl comes over here, and yuh put it in her head that she should go to an English school. Ye're the one who should explain yourself."

Lebeuf relaxed. "So what? Gisèle wants to go on studying and her parents can't afford it..."

"Don't play innocent, Jules Lebeuf. Some little girl who don't know nothin'about nothin'comes around, and yuh take her to the West End to get her a job, then yuh want to get her into an English school. And without her mother knowing anything about it. Then yuh say 'so what?' It just isn't done. If I was her mother I wouldn't be happy either..."

"How do you know she's not happy?"

"How do I know it? Estelle herself came to the restaurant and told me about it."

Jules tapped his coat pocket where he had put Gisèle's test. Mrs. Lafrenière's opposition could become disastrous.

With a look of satisfaction, Margot tossed back a lock of hair that curled down on her forehead. "Estelle is a lady," she said. "She didn't say much, but I can read between the lines."

"I'm not asking for your comments. What did she say?"

"She said to leave the girl alone."

"Leave the girl... Dammit! Bill himself asked me to give her the bloody test, and now the old lady..."

"Wait a minute. That's not the way she said it. She didn't say,'I want Mr. Lebeuf to leave the girl alone,' but that's what she meant, as true as I'm standin' here in front of yuh. She didn't want to hurt yer feelings naturally. She

195

knows that yuh and Bill get along well together."

Lebeuf shook his head in disgust. "All right, we'll see."

Margot cuddled up to him. "I know yuh didn't mean no wrong. The girl came moping around here, yuh took her maybe a little too seriously, and then..."

"Leave me alone, will you?" Jules pulled himself away, grabbed his jacket in one hand, his briefcase in the other, and went out, slamming the door behind him.

XV

Lebeuf put his lunchbox on the seat and glanced at his watch. Bill should be getting here in five minutes, at nine-thirty. Since Bouboule lived in this district, they would have time to pay him a visit and come back by midnight. Jules sat down and sighed. The empty shack offered a depressing sight. For the first time in eighteen months, Jules noticed the smoked-up windows, the grayish walls smeared with fingerprints, the big lightbulb hanging from its wire like a spider, the long table scarred by knife cuts. He buried his head in his hands and tried to think.

It had been a bad day. After his discussion with Margot, he had walked over to the university hoping to find Weston. But the American had not shown up. After his lectures, instead of going to meet Gisèle on her way out of the convent school, as he had promised himself, he had ended up in a tavern with a group of his classmates. He thought that perhaps it would be better to see Bill first. Mrs. Lafrenière's visit to Margot worried him. Were they thinking once more of sending Gisèle to the factory? Suddenly he thought of Bouboule again. That was something even more pressing. In what condition would they find the old man? And what arrangement would he himself make with regard to Stevens' offer? Jules absent-mindedly rubbed his cheek; it was still swollen but the pain had almost disappeared.

Bill's arrival interrupted his meditation. "Hey, Lebeuf, how's it goin'?"

At the same moment the fat cashier stuck his head through the wicket. "Have you got shares in the company, Bill? Comin' in at nine-thirty to start work?"

"Get back into yer cage, goddam monkey!" snapped Bill. "Yuh can be sure that I didn't come to work ahead of time to see yer pig's face."

But Lafrenière seemed to forget about the cashier immediately. He walked toward Lebeuf and put his hand on his shoulder. "How's it goin', Lebeuf, goin' okay eh?"

"Hey, Bill. Not bad."

The student recalled the sweepers' mysterious attitude since his visit with Stevens. He had not had time to think it over. "We'd do just as well to walk there. It'll loosen up our legs."

Bill nodded and they went out. A gust of cold air lashed against their faces. Shoving their hands into their pockets, they walked through an immense, brick-laid yard, over a tangle of shining tracks. Overhead ran a network of trolley cables. A little further, to the left, were the gaping doors of the barns where the cars were entering with metallic screeches.

Dressed in old corduroy pants and an orange woolen sweater, which replaced his work clothes, Bill was moving along with his head down, not looking at the student. The imprint of the cap he had just taken off still showed like a crown on his thin, yellowish hair. His toothless gums were munching constantly as if he were sucking on an everlasting candy. Lebeuf, a head taller than he, trudged by his side, his neck sunk in the collar of his pullover.

"I've been thinking about that business of your girl," he said after a period of silence.

"Yeah?" The mood was reticent. They walked another

fifteen paces without exchanging a word. A siren wailed on the river side. "Yeah, so what do yuh think about it?"

"I've been thinking about a compromise," said Lebeuf. "I don't know what you're gonna think about it. A compromise which looks as if it might straighten out both problems. But I suppose you've already heard about it?"

Bill stopped sucking on his imaginary candy. "A compromise? Whattya mean by that?"

"Well, I was thinking that Gisèle could find a part-time job and take night courses."

Bill did not look surprised. "A job and study at the same time? Do kids like Gisèle do that?"

"The Québécois kids don't do it often, but you see it all the time with English kids."

Bill scratched his head with his calloused hand and dirty fingernails. "Yeah, well, that's what they say. "He did not seem enthusiastic about the idea. "Yeah, and where would she go for these courses?"

Lebeuf mentioned Sir George Williams.

"Yeah." Bill began to suck on his tongue again. "That's a good college, eh?" Clearly, he was asking the question just to stall for time.

"It's no worse than the others," said Lebeuf.

Bill scratched his head again. A long silence followed. "I' m gonna tell yuh, Lebeuf, English and all that — it's all very nice — but as far as I'm concerned, that English stuff..." A gesture completed his thought.

Jules let a few seconds pass. "If you want Gisèle to continue her studies, it's because you want her to come out all right afterwards, you want her to land a good job, right?"

"Yeah, that's the way it is, I guess."

"It's not easy without English, unless you're gonna do hard work. And Gisèle doesn't seem to me to be one of the strongest . . ."

"No, as far as strength goes, she's not too strong, that's true. She never was very strong." However Bill did not seem to be convinced. He was turning a more serious objection over in his mind. "And what are we gonna do if all of a sudden, she falls for one of them blokes?" he asked after a pause.

Lebeuf raised his hand as if to say that it was only a vague possibility.

"It's happened before," Bill affirmed with animation. "Don't tell me it hasn't happened; it's happened. There was a girl who lived not far from me when I was a kid. She fell for a big English bloke and believe it or not, she married him, yessir! I don't have to tell you that it raised a goddamn big stink. Her ol' man, by Christ, went right through the roof. I wouldn't like that to happen at my place. You haven't got a daughter, but if yuh had a daughter, how would yuh like it if she married an English bloke?"

"I dunno," said Lebeuf. "Maybe I wouldn't like it, but it's all pure speculation."

"It's happened," Bill repeated stubbornly, "it's happened. Gisèle, she's not bad looking at all. An'I say that not just because she's my girl. Yuh seen her. She's only sixteen and the guys are already hanging around. Thicker than flies." He held ten fingers up in front of him. "Yessir!"

Jules pictured again the pale, tired, yet young and attractive face of Gisèle as she had thanked him three days earlier. "Yes she's very beautiful."

Bill stuck out his chest. "It's not because she's my own, but she's a far cry from being an old moth-eaten hag."

Lebeuf felt uneasy. Would it not be better to leave things the way they were, drop the whole business. But he thought about the test he had in his pocket. *I can't let her down*. He found himself asking, almost in spite of himself, "The guys you said were hanging around, would you like one of them as a son-in-law?"

Bill seemed embarrassed. He rolled his tongue several times in his mouth and swished saliva. "I'm gonna tell yuh, Lebeuf. Me, I'm just a sweeper. I didn't want to go to school, and the old man wasn't about to push me. I'm not complaining. I am what I am. But if there was some way to do it, I'd like for Gisèle to have something a li'l better. I haven't got fancy ideas or anything, but I'd like her to have it better than me, I don't know, a good clean job, then marry a guy with a bit of education, a guy who can stand on his own two feet..."

He was tempted to add *A guy like you*. But he held back. Lebeuf was not interested in marriage. The proof — he was going out with Marguerite. Bill had his own idea. *If he's going out with her, it's because she's coming across pretty well*. Bill himself would not have minded having her in his bed. She was a bit on the plump side, but it was good, healthy, firm flesh. You didn't have to poke her to know that. Lebeuf knew his onions. And if he decided to marry later, he would still be a good husband. He was a solid guy. You could depend on him. "Anyhow, I'm gonna think about it, Lebeuf. I'm not sayin' yes, and I'm not sayin' no."

Bill seemed reassured. His guilty look had disappeared. Why had he let himself be influenced by Charlot and the others? Lebeuf had lost his job, but so what? Jules was not a sweeper like the others. A job like that, better than that even — he just had to lift his finger and he would find a dozen. And it was true that if he had lost this one, it was because of the others, the sweepers, because he had tried to stick up for them. That was a dirty business... Bill remembered why they had come out. That poor

Bouboule. He was the one who had gotten the dirty end of the stick. It must have been a hard blow.

"One thing I didn't mention to you," said Lebeuf.

"Yeah, what is it?"

"I had Gisèle take a test, a real one."

"You mean the other night."

"No, a test with a psychologist. You've heard about it. It's to measure aptitudes, see what a person can do in such and such a field..."

"Yeah? So?"

"Gisèle has a gift for mathematics, no doubt about it. She could probably go far."

Bill rubbed his hands with an air of satisfaction. "She's bright all right. Me, I was a damned clod in school, but she's quite bright."

"Does that mean that you want her to go on with her studies?"

Bill stopped to roll a cigarette. He licked the paper sloppily, then struck a match. "I'll tell yuh, Lebeuf, education, I'm for it one hundred percent. Only an English school, now that's another kettle of fish, yuh see."

"It wouldn't mean that she'd lose her language," said Lebeuf.

"That's what they say, she wouldn't lose her language, but I'm not so sure. With a kid like Gisèle yuh can't be sure. Young people like to do what the others are doing."

A vivid image of Gisèle flashed into Lebeuf's mind — her dark impish eyes, her frail neck with the tiny blue veins, her fair skin, her smile... Was Bill right? Was she as fragile morally as physically? Her escapade with Sillery seemed to point in that direction. *I'm being unfair*. Going out with Augustin was one thing, becoming anglicized was another. Jules was tempted to explain to the sweeper that the program of studies at Sir George Williams, where Gisèle could specialize in mathematics from

202

the start, would be more profitable to her than a program built on Latin and composition for which she showed no aptitude. But Bill would not understand. *I must see Gisèle again and discuss it with her.*

XVI

Bill had hardly exaggerated when he had said Bouboule's house was a shack. It was a small, wooden building, covered with sooty, peeling paint that gave the impression of an alligator's skin. The pinewood balcony was rotten and the creaking stairs leaned a good fifteen degrees. Pieces of cardboard replaced the glass panes on the front door. The doorbell did not work. When Lebeuf turned the lever, only the screech of rusted gears was heard.

"Let's go in just the same," said Bill. "I'm sure he's in. There's a light inside."

The door was not locked. Lebeuf pushed it with his shoulder. The stuffy smell of old pipesmoke caught his nose. He found himself in a corridor with yellowish walls, dimly lit by a small bulb which hung from the ceiling. At the far end, there was a stairway leading to the second floor. The first room on the right was empty.

"Bouboule," shouted Bill, "are yuh there?" There was no answer.

They walked toward the back into the kitchen. There the door was blocked by a cast-iron stove. Everything seemed to indicate that this was the only occupied room in the house. In the dusk, his little ostrich head completely upright over his thin neck, Bouboule sat motionless in his rocker. His hands were resting flat on his knees. Only the continuous twitch of his Adam's apple showed that he was not dead.

204

"Bouboule, hell, how come you don't answer when somebody calls."

The old man slowly turned his head. "Oh, it's you, Bill, and Lebeuf. Sit down," he said in his weak, raspy, toneless voice, as if he had been expecting their visit.

As he moved closer, Jules was stunned by the change in Bouboule's face after only three days. He seemed even skinnier than before. The muscles of his neck stuck out from under his skin. His cheeks were hollow. But most of all his blank stare, his haggard look, his lifeless eyes were a sad sight.

"How are things, Bouboule?" Lebeuf inquired cordially.

Bouboule seemed to come out of his lethargy. He pulled a letter out of his shirt pocket which he stuck under his visitors' noses. "The goddamned sons of bitches think they've got me, but they won't get me!" His voice kept the same monotone, regardless of the meaning of the words.

"What do yuh mean?"

Bouboule shook the letter once more. "They think I'm gonna crawl over to their office to get a damned check they're giving me 'for past services rendered.' Here, Lebeuf, you read this out loud. They're gonna stuff it up their bigshots' arses for quite a goddamned while before they see me around, You read that out loud there, Lebeuf."

The student took the wrinkled piece of paper, smudged with fingerprints, which Bouboule must have read over a dozen times.

"Come on, let's hear it."

Jules drew closer to a small round lamp on the sideboard, and read:

Dear Sir,

In recognition of past services rendered, we, the mana-

205

gers of the Metropolitan Transport Company, have decided to grant you a check in the amount of six hundred and twenty-eight dollars ($628.00) covering a six-month salary period.

Could you please present yourself at our head office at your convenience...

" 'At your convenience!' You hear that, Bill?'' The old man was shaking with rage. Bill stared at him in surprise.

...at your convenience between nine-thirty and twelve, to receive the above-mentioned check and sign the necessary forms.

The letter ended there. Jules stopped.

"Read it to the end."

"But that's it, that's all there is."

The old man waved his hand. "No, no, read it all, right to the bottom of the page, I want Bill to hear that."

Jules picked up the letter again and read, somewhat surprised.

Your obedient servants,
      The Managers of the Metropolitan Transport
      Company
      per: Robert Stevens

Bouboule appeared to be on the verge of a nervous breakdown. His arms were flailing left and right as if he had become demented. "Christ, did you hear that, Bill? Did you, Lebeuf? 'Your obedient servants.' I have cleaned their shitty trams for the last thirty-three years — thirty-three years the day before yesterday — and now they're *my* obedient servants." The old man dropped his arms and reassumed his rigid; comatose position. "If there's a God up above, he won't let things like this

206

happen." Now there was a quiver in his voice. "He won't let dirty things like this happen."

Lebeuf and Bill looked at each other with despair. Jules felt explanations would be useless. Bouboule would not understand, especially in his present state.

"I would offer you something, boys," said the old man still motionless and staring blankly, "but I drank all the beer I had last night."

"Not necessary," said Lebeuf raising a hand. He shook his head imperceptibly. The lines on his face became rigid for a second. Then he said very softly, "Listen Bouboule, we went over to see Stevens, two mornings ago, Charlot, Pop Breton and myself..."

The old man turned his head and questioned Lebeuf with his eyes. "There might be a way to fix it all up..."

Bill looked at Lebeuf with reproach. Why give Bouboule false hopes? It would only make him more disillusioned in the end.

"There is a way to fix it up, yet there's a catch in it..."

Bouboule was soaking up the student's words. Jules hesitated. *Now Bouboule is my friend, but as soon as he finds out, that'll be it. For him and for Bill, as well as for the rest of the men, I'll stand on the other side of the fence.* And that was not all. If he took on the job of foreman, what would become of his free student's life, his literary dreams? Would they vanish?

"Hell, what's the catch," asked Bill, unable to contain himself any longer. Bouboule, for his part, seemed hypnotized. Head forward, his Adam's apple now stationary, his eyes fixed on Lebeuf.

"Stevens is ready to take you back, Bouboule," said Lebeuf slowly, "after a three-month suspension. He's even ready to transfer Lévêque... But, the only thing is, he wants me to take the job as foreman. I handled it as best I could. There was nothing else to be done. No way he wanted to change his mind on that."

He stopped talking to look at Bouboule and his jaw dropped with surprise. Big tears slowly ran down the old man's furrowed cheeks. Bill was vigorously rubbing his nose with the back of his hand.

"You did that for me, Lebeuf! I've got two boys I brought up here, in this here house, that I never even see, and you, Lebeuf, you did that for me!" Bouboule got up and hugged the student with his bony arms. "If there's a God above, he won't forget this, Lebeuf."

Jules pulled away slowly. He did not deserve such a display of gratitude. After all, the arrangement probably was to his own advantage. Why had he hemmed and hawed so much? He sat Bouboule down gently. "Yeah, well, we're gonna let you rest a little," he said. "Bill and I have got to go back to the shack." He took long strides toward the door, and Bill followed him.

XVII

Lebeuf was coming out of his philology class, when he saw Weston. Contrary to his habit, the American was not wearing his khaki pants and army tunic. A beige gabardine suit — apparently new — a bow tie and polished shoes made him look almost comical. He wore a bandage over his right brow.

"Hi," said Lebeuf. He had not seen Ken since the brawl at La Bougrine. Each time he had phoned, Thérèse had sharply answered that the American was absent.

"Hi." Weston pulled his friend slightly away from the other students and asked if he could come to the Anchor at eight-thirty.

"The Anchor? Yes, sure, I'm not working tonight. You've hit the jackpot?"

The Anchor was one of Montreal's plush cabarets. Its dining room had been ostentatiously decorated to look like the inside of a great ocean liner.

"It's a quiet place," explained Weston. "Eight-thirty, don't forget."

Jules nodded as the American left in a hurry.

At precisely eight-thirty, Jules stepped down the spiral staircase that led to the Underwater Room of the Anchor Club. He walked past a hulking doorman, dressed as a quartermaster, who stood, chest out, at the bottom of the stairs. He noticed Weston seated at a table in the back, close to an enormous anchor hanging from the wall. He stepped up his pace.

"Takin' it easy, aren't you?" he said.

On the tablecloth, in front of the American, stood a bottle of Bordeaux in a little basin of ice. To the left, by a red candle, a saucer with the coat of arms of the King of England held the remains of a Saint Honoré cake.

"I decided to have dinner here at the last minute," said Weston. "Otherwise I would have invited you." He switched to English, "Waiter, another glass."

Ken wore the same suit he had worn that afternoon. His usually disheveled blond hair was stuck down close to his skull with hair cream. Lebeuf sat down, intrigued. Weston filled his friend's glass. "I'm going back to St. Louis on the midnight train," he said, looking at his glass.

Jules swallowed a bit of wine. "You're not serious? Five weeks before the end of classes! And what about your thesis?"

"The wastepaper basket." Weston took some wine, too. "You see, I'm fed up with all this. What happened at La Bougrine was the final straw. The next day, Thérèse did not want to say a word to me. She had this woebegone look. I tried to explain things to her. Nothing for it. So I took a place in a rooming house. Then I said to myself, 'What are you doing here in Canada? To hell with it all.' I stuffed all my papers into the basket and kept only my little notebook of words and expressions." He tapped his pocket with the tip of his finger. "I've got this anyway. It's not so bad."

"Yeah." Lebeuf was rolling his glass between his hairy hands. This departure was a hard blow for him. Ken was his only true friend. The other students were too young, and there was no way to talk to Sillery. Besides, since the other night's incident, they only nodded to each other coldly. "Well, you know what you've gotta do. When you get right down to it, I can't blame you."

"Can you see writing a thesis on French Canadians in order to become a reporter in the States?"

"Yeah, of course..." That's what Lebeuf himself had told him repeatedly. He poured himself another glass which he sipped slowly. "Still, I would have liked you to publish that!"

Weston looked flattered. "Don't make me laugh!"

"I'm not joking! *Sketches of French-Canadian Life,* with true-to-life scenes, your personal impressions. It would have done us good, it would have gotten us out of our shells. Of course the bigwigs at the university wouldn't have gone for it."

"I couldn't care less." Ken was drinking his wine in small sips, daydreaming. He ordered a second bottle, then turned to his friend. "Why don't you come to St. Louis with me?"

Lebeuf raised a hand. "Out of the question."

"It would be a change for you."

Lebeuf shook his head. *Must I tell him I'm gonna become a foreman?* The news now seemed unimportant. He could not tell him about Gisèle either. He might have mentioned it at another time, incidentally dropped a word during a conversation. But now Weston was leaving. He would not see him again. Lebeuf would remain alone.

"I'd be happy if you came," said Weston.

"Yes, I know, so would I..."

The big man's eyes wandered through the underwater room. A long-haired pianist, who sat at the keyboard in an alcove shaped more-or-less like an oyster shell, began a Strauss waltz. A brunette and a blonde, wearing very chic, low-cut dresses and smelling of perfume, brushed by their table, laughing very loudly. They sat down at the next table.

211

Weston appeared happy with the diversion, emotion having threatened to make their conversation ridiculous. "How much do you think they charge?" he asked.

Returning from far away, Jules shrugged his shoulders. "No idea. You could always ask them." He was not interested in that kind of affair for the moment.

Weston frowned indifferently. "That type make you pay for the frills too."

Lebeuf smiled pensively. "Is it easy in St. Louis?"

"You can manage," answered Weston. ' 'Going to clubs. Sometimes it doesn't cost you anything. A few drinks. You've also got the black districts, but that's a little more dangerous."

Jules thought about his stay in Boston. Once in a tavern he had picked up a big blonde who reeked of sweat. "Everywhere the same," he said.

"Yes, everywhere the same," repeated Weston. "You go to Europe, the army, the occupation; it's the same everywhere."

The two women had stopped laughing. They were looking at the bar in a blasé manner.

"Pardon me, Madame, did you inadvertently drop this silken glove?" Lebeuf was startled. Sillery's voice! He clenched his fists. Why had Weston invited him, especially after the fight the other night?

The two ladies giggled. "What is he saying?" they said in English.

"Four fingers, a t'umb, I am under ze impression that eet ees a glove." Augustin's voice in English, which he spoke with a thick accent, sounded even more artificial.

The ladies were now roaring with laughter. "Isn't he cute?"

Augustin curtly placed the glove on the table. He was not pleased with the compliment. Then he walked toward Weston, hand extended. "Gentleman, I am tearing myself away from that soft tropical flesh to fly toward your polar bottle." After he had shaken hands with the American, Augustin turned to Lebeuf. "Whom do I see? Is it not the legendary hero, under whose valiant blows — if my memory serves me right — the columns of the Bougrinal temple collapsed?"

Weston smiled. "Augustin, I'll really miss you. Believe me," he said in English.

Sillery did not understand. "You're leaving?"

"Yessir."

Throwing his arms up in distress, Augustin sat down, as if he had forgotten to shake Lebeuf's hand. "What do I hear? Son of proud America, would you nurture, *de vero*, within the recesses of your powerful mind, the ominous intention of leaving the charming solitudes of our small burg for the deceitful pleasures of southern cities?"

"On the midnight train," said Weston.

"Cruel gods, is it possible?" The news was a shock to him. He hesitated for a while. "Allow me, gentlemen, to reinvigorate my shaken spirits with the consoling lips of this amphora."

He grabbed the bottle by the neck and drank a mouthful. He then touched his lips with his batiste handkerchief. "And now enough of joking. To arms! Lebeuf, noble warrior, deftly bring forward a straitjacket to save this foolish young man from the claws..."

Jules cut him off. "Weston's leaving tonight, and that is all you have to say?" Lebeuf immediately got angry with himself for the outburst. It was stupid. He was not going to start a hassle under such circumstances.

"Really?" replied Sillery. "I hadn't noticed. Thank you for the information."

The conversation languished for a while. As a going-away party, it lacked spirit. Weston said that once he got to St. Louis, he would try to land a job on a newspaper at

$35.00 a week. Afterwards, if he was lucky and his articles were successful, he would try his hand with the chain publications, and in five or ten years he would be able to live like a lord.

"A veritable El Dorado," Augustin remarked.

The flight of Weston was causing his own young wings to flutter. The wind was making his nostrils flare. He would lift himself "over the ranges, over the valleys," he would cross the great frog pond, that modern Mediterranean. Even the jungles of Africa would not hinder his adventurous steps.

Lebeuf shook his head and poured another glass. *My last get-together with Weston and look how it's going.* Actually, it was perhaps just as well. What can one say under such circumstances?

"Yeah. Well, as far as I'm concerned, I'm gonna keep on cleaning the shit out of my streetcars," he declared.

"You've chosen the best course to follow," Augustin exclaimed. "Let us cultivate our excrement — it's the salt of the earth."

"You're going to continue at the Transport Company even after your degree?" asked Weston.

Lebeuf lifted his hand lazily. "Why not? Degrees, they're not good for much."

Weston nodded his head. "Yeah! That's for sure." Still, he thought that Lebeuf was exaggerating. "What do you think of it, Augustin?"

Sillery, whose eyes were following the movements of a young waiter, turned smartly toward his companions. "Gentlemen, I look at you and I admire you. Indomitable strugglers-for-life, you are launching yourselves into your respective careers with the ardor of a frothing Pegasus who . . ."

Weston nodded his head.

"Yeah!"

214

The waiter had just disappeared through the kitchen door. Augustin resumed, raising his forefinger. "One of you will brandish the torch of journalism to enlighten the pulp-eaters about fires, the disappearance of dogs, bargains in underwear, the indispositions of actresses, daily horoscopes and other crucial events of contemporary living. What is more noble, gentlemen, what is more admirable than thus to propagate culture and a taste for the beautiful in the working masses, than to sow the good word..."

The waiter reappeared, a tray in his hand. Augustin stopped him as he passed. "Would you be kind enough to fetch me a chicken sandwich, grilled, as well as some pont-neuf potatoes?"

"You forgot something" said Weston with a big smile.

Sillery went on the defensive. "And what might that be, pray tell."

"You forgot the sex crimes and holdups. Without them the newspapers would be pretty flat."

Augustin relaxed. *"Lapsus mnemonis,* my dear, for which I am deeply distressed. Unfortunately, such crimes do not take place every day. That would be too convenient. Journalists would have no more value. The *ne plus ultra* of journalism, as we all know, is to produce articles *ex nihilo."*

"In that case, you should be doing it," said Lebeuf.

The dandy pursed his lips and retorted in a falsetto voice. "You flatter me, my dear, I feel incapable of pursuing activities on many fronts, as you do."

"As I do?"

Augustin wet his lips with his glass and went on in a satisfied tone. "Indeed. On the one hand scouring the Augean stables which house the streetcars of our metropolis, on the other undertaking the Balzacian labors of writing novels."

Lebeuf's features darkened. "I don't see what Balzac has to do with it. I..."

Weston interrupted him. "The last drink, gentlemen. Must toddle along. You're going to miss your potatoes, Augustin."

His glass drained, he gave the signal to leave. It was twenty-to-twelve, and it took at least ten minutes to get to Windsor Station.

A fine rain accompanied by gusts of wind swept across Dominion Square. Conversation was almost impossible. *So much the better* thought Lebeuf. *What can you say to a friend who is going away, forever undoubtedly?*

He pulled the collar of his raincoat up around his huge head. Even Sillery remained silent. A few passersby hugged the walls as they rushed forward. Soon the massive silhouette of the station with its pointed turrets appeared in front of them. They went in.

The hall of lost steps. A gray expanse lighted by enormous chandeliers, the vague impression of a cathedral. Employees were selling tickets and giving out information. A policeman was walking back and forth swinging his nightstick. Some travelers were rushing toward their cars. Others, surrounded by little groups of relatives and friends, were exchanging odd remarks or risking jokes without fear of repercussion. They were undoubtedly leaving for long periods.

Ken had no time to waste. His train was leaving in five minutes.

"You'll keep in touch," said Lebeuf.

"You bet. As soon as I become famous," said Weston, walking quickly.

After a rapid handshake, he got into the car. Neither Lebeuf nor Sillery thought it appropriate to wait on the platform until the train got underway. They walked slowly in the opposite direction. Jules was looking for an

216

excuse to get away as soon as possible.

As they entered the hall of the lost steps, Sillery dropped a remark. "Still, it's going to leave an empty spot, Weston's going away..."

Surprised, Lebeuf looked him straight in the eye. Augustin was really moved, too, in his own way. "If you've got nothing to do," said Jules, "maybe we could go and have a drink before going to bed."

"An inspired idea! We could return to our distinguished ladies at the Anchor. I'm sure that they inadvertently dropped another glove. We could pick it up."

"No, not there," said Lebeuf, "it's stifling."

"Well, I know a cathouse where one can pass the night comfortably — good fire, good lodgings... and all the rest."

"Does it tempt you?" asked Lebeuf.

"Not especially. It's the simple suggestion of an old horse worn out under the harness."

"Then let's just dig up a quiet little bar without anything to distract us."

They left the station together. The rain was still falling, a liquid dust which wet the face in one swipe, like a wet cloth. Lebeuf hunched his huge shoulders to face the gusts. Sillery was not a bad sort after all. You simply had to accept him as he was.

XVIII

Lebeuf stopped in front of the Sainte Sophie convent school. It was a large building of smoke-darkened brick. Along the lenght of the roof ran a copper ledge surmounted by wrought-iron curlicues. In the façade, on a stone tablet, an inscription was written: J.M.J. 1898 A.D. Jules lit a cigarette and took a few steps in the direction of the school yard. From the window on the first floor came the voices of young girls repeating their lessons. It was a beautiful day. Only a few clouds, transparent like puffs of pipe smoke, disrupted the blue of the sky. Jules adjusted his tie and passed his finger inside the starched collar which was rubbing his neck. In a quarter of an hour, Gisèle would come out and walk toward him. He would show her the results of the test. Together they would discuss her future… Lebeuf, who had waited four days to come, was now burning with impatience. *Why did I wait so long? It's stupid.* Bill did not understand anything about anything. And the mother seemed to be worse still — badgering Margot at the restaurant to get it across to him that he should leave the girl alone. *All they had to do was not bother me in the first place. Now I have to see it through.* Gisèle herself would certainly understand…

A chirping of shrill voices startled him. Calling to each other, a group of schoolgirls were scrambling down the stairs. Lebeuf came closer to the main fence. There were so many girls that he was afraid of missing Gisèle. But

218

suddenly he saw her. She was coming down the stone stairs slowly, swinging a bundle of books at the end of the strap. Her three-quarter coat, tightened to size by a wide black belt, seemed too big for her. *Perhaps it's her aunt's or her mother's old coat.* Lebeuf was moved by the thought. *What's the matter with me? Nothing would be more natural.*

Suddenly Gisèle's name rang out on the staircase. She turned to wait for two other schoolgirls, then began to chat with them. Lebeuf retired a few paces. This was upsetting his plans. But he refused to back out from the meeting. *After all, it's the only way to see her.* With an air of indifference, he moved toward the threesome. At that moment, Gisèle caught sight of him. She stopped in the middle of a sentence and stood with her mouth open, her black eyes fixed on Lebeuf.

"Hello," said Lebeuf, making a gesture as if to shake her hand.

"Hello, Mr. Lebeuf."

Gisèle blushed, swinging her books in front of her at the end of the strap, then made the introductions. "Mr. Lebeuf, this is Jeanne Lesieur and Pauline Cantin, my school friends."

The two young girls ogled the big man, then exchanged knowing smiles.

"You've come to speak to me, Mr. Lebeuf?"

Jules nodded.

The other two schoolgirls moved away. "See you tomorrow, Gisèle."

"Yes, till tomorrow then."

The man and the girl walked for a while in silence. The sun was beginning to set, projecting notches of shadow on the asphalt road. Wrought-iron staircases hung from the fronts of buildings. A few cyclists, bent over their handle bars, passed by, pedaling vigorously. The siren of an

219

ambulance could be heard in the distance. Gisèle, her head held straight, her cheeks still rosy, swung her books at arm's length. Her beret and the waves of black hair escaping from it gave her the look of a small child.

"Maybe it wasn't a good idea to come and wait for you like this," said Lebeuf.

"Oh no. Why? It was fine. I..."

She lifted her eyes rapidly towards him. Lebeuf noticed for the first time the shape of her eyebrows, which slanted slightly toward the temples, giving her an oriental look. The lithograph of Natasha came into his mind again.

Gisèle lowered her head. "I thought that I'd see you again before today."

Lebeuf felt a twinge of pleasure. She had been anxious to see him again? Was it possible?

"The test — I didn't pass it, I suppose."

Lebeuf's spirits fell. *It was only because of the test, obviously.*

"You more than passed it. You placed among the top five percent."

Gisèle eyes twinkled with pleasure. Then her eyes fixed on Jules and she was seized with doubt. "You don't look pleased."

"Not pleased? On the contrary, I'm very pleased. Why do you say that?"

"I don't know. It just seemed to me that..."

"I'm just surprised that Bill didn't tell you about the test. I told him all about it the day before yesterday."

Gisèle turned away. Her father had deliberately kept quiet. She looked absent-mindedly at the gray mass of the Radium Institute with its balustrated balcony.

"We can go into a restaurant, if you like," said Lebeuf. "It would be quieter."

They went into an old restaurant with walls covered in panels of embossed sheet-metal. The table tops, wiped hastily, still showed the marks made by the dishcloth. Lebeuf looked at Gisèle, but she seemed to see nothing. She slipped quickly into one of the shoddy booths. The bluish light of the wall fixtures accentuated her pale complexion.

"So I passed it then, the big test?" she said, trying to make her voice sound natural.

"You had doubts?"

"I don't know. All kinds of things were running through my head. It didn't seem hard when I was doing it, but I figured there were probably a few trick questions."

"There probably were, for those who don't have the aptitude. Without being advanced mathematics, the test..."

"Ah. So it wasn't advanced mathematics. Do you think I'd be able to do that?"

"Probably. Of course, you never know until you try, but the test gives a pretty good indication. It's better than in literature, where you're never sure of anything."

The big man ran his hand through his reddish crew-cut.

"But that doesn't matter. That's not what we're talking about."

Gisèle looked inquiringly at the student. "Is it only literature that you're interested in?"

"Why do you say that?"

Gisèle hesitated a few seconds. "When you came to our place... my compositions were the first thing you looked at. You didn't find them good... and I thought..."

"Yeah. I was wrong. You see, when you're really interested in something you tend to ignore everything else. Me, for instance. I'm twenty-nine years old, I'm still studying, and I work like a... I've got a job at the streetcar barns. I'm not doing too well for my age." He stopped abruptly, surprised at his own expansiveness.

"But aren't you going to be a foreman now?"

221

Jules rubbed his chin with an air of indecision. "Yeah, probably."

"And you're not pleased? It's because of Bouboule that..."

Lebeuf shook his head. Coming from anyone else but Gisèle the question would have annoyed him. "Yeah, probably because of that."

Gisèle was watching him with her large, warm eyes, and Lebeuf suddenly felt the need to explain himself more fully. "Do you understand, Gisèle, how a guy can spend his life looking for something, trying to express something, not knowing if he's ever going to succeed of if he has any talent at all? And because of that, how a guy can neglect everything else — like making money, getting a good job, getting married maybe, living like other people? Can you understand that?"

Gisèle fidgeted on her chair. She seemed to be thinking. "Yes," she said. "I think that I can understand that."

Lebeuf had a feeling of joy. *She understands me.* He made a motion to take the schoolgirl's hand. Gisèle pretended not to notice and swallowed three spoonfuls of ice cream quickly.

Lebeuf pulled himself together. "Well, that's not what we're talking about. You know the results of your test. You're the one it concerns. Your chances of succeeding in maths are excellent. The sooner you begin the better. There's no French girls' school for you to go to, so it seems to me that Sir George Williams is the only place. You'll have to make up your own mind."

Gisèle began to scrape the floor with the toe of her shoe, as she had done during the meeting at the home. "Myself, I want to very much... Only, an English school... That doesn't go over too well at my house."

"You couldn't try to explain it to them?"

Gisèle shrugged her shoulders. "Me? You know they don't listen to what I say."

"Yeah."

"You, Mr. Lebeuf, couldn't you...?"

"Not likely."

With Bill, yes, perhaps. But not with Mrs. Lafrenière. Jules had to hold himself back from telling Gisèle to run away from home, to defy her parents. *No, I couldn't tell her to do that.*

"If I push too much, then it would be worse," he said.

Gisèle sighed, and Lebeuf lifted his head. He was shaken by the expression on the young girl's face. Her hands clasped over the edge of the table, she was biting her lips, and her eyes were dim with tears.

"Listen," he said. "Maybe we can work something out."

The scene at Bouboule's place is repeating itself he thought. *But there, at least, there was a solution, whereas here...*

"Work something out? How?" asked Gisèle, a ray of hope in her eyes.

"I don't know yet. I'll have to think about it."

He would let her know as soon as he found a way. For her part, Gisèle was to call him if there was anyting new.

It was time to leave. The young girl got up. *I can't even take her home* thought Lebeuf. In front of the restaurant he held out his hand. "Good-bye."

"Good-bye."

She turned and rushed off in the direction of Pius IX Boulevard. Her books swung gently at the end of the strap. Jules watched her disappear at the corner of the street, then, looking worried, he went into a tavern.

XIX

Lebeuf got up at four-twenty. It was time for his new round.

The Hochelaga waiting room was a depressing sight at night. The rough, dark woodwork ran along the walls at elbow height; above, heavy-set frames outlined huge rectangles in yellowish plaster. A few yellowed posters hung from a greenish felt bulletin board. Bulbs, dressed with hexagonal shades, threw a stark light that hurt the eyes over the room. In the far corner, the big, bald-headed cashier was poking away on his adding machine. The room itself was deserted.

With a yawn, Lebeuf stretched his arms, straightened his leather-peaked cap on his head and ran his fingers over the gold buttons of his foreman's uniform. Then he picked up his electric lantern and his keyring and trudged toward the door. The autumn sky was overcast. Thick, notched clouds were scudding by the October moon. It was cold. Soon, the first snow would surely begin to fall. Jules hung his head and walked toward the car barn.

He had been at his job for six months, and his predictions were holding true. The sweepers, his old partners, had slowly turned away from him. At first, when Bouboule's reinstallation and their pay raise were still fresh in their memories — Stevens had finally agreed to suspend Bouboule only for one month — the men had been warm toward their young foreman. Work was done well and quickly — Jules had almost nothing to do. Then, bit by bit, as time went by, they had forgotten. They had begun to consider Lebeuf as a boss. Work had become sloppy. Veiled complaints about the job had resumed, more loudly than before. The young supervisor had been forced to become more vigilant. He did not have a choice; anybody else in his situation would have shown himself more demanding. He asked for nothing more than the bare minimum; infinitely less than what Lévêque had required. But he could not stand playing chain-gang leader. On many occasions he had been tempted to hand in his resignation.

Yet no violent conflict had broken out. Once, in an effort to effect a rapprochement, Lebeuf had showed up at the shack for lunch break with his lunchbox. The sweepers had said nothing. Some had looked at him with suspicion, even hostility. Then they had simply gobbled down their sandwiches and gone out without a word, before the usual time. Since then, Jules had eaten alone in the waiting room, sometimes bandying comments with the cashier or an inspector who happened to come in to warm up in between cars.

On another occasion, as Lebeuf was walking in the car barn, he had heard voices and peals of laughter coming from the inside of a tram. He had walked over and seen Bouboule looking exasperated and facing up to the crew of sweepers. During the first weeks after his return, the old man had been left alone. But now, he had once again become the butt of his cronies' jokes. The taunts were much more cutting now because, since the incident that had almost cost him his job, Bouboule had been acting as a model employee.

"Have yuh got shares in the company, Bouboule, to be such an eager beaver?" asked Charlot.

"Maybe he wants to have Lévêque's job and become

the foreman,'' quipped another, amid a ripple of laughter.

Bouboule was frothing with helpless rage. ''If you're a bunch of goddamn pigs, and if you leave your cars full of shit, it's your business,'' he retorted in his little raspy voice.

A burst of anger stirred Lebeuf. He was on the verge of jumping into the car. But another voice was raised. This time Bill was the scapegoat for doing a conscientious job.

''Ain't it right, what I heard? That yuh wanna go to college in the fall, Bill? Who knows, it could be useful to yuh some day.'' That one was meant for Lebeuf. They knew that they both met at the tavern once in a while.

Fortunately, Bill had answered with aplomb. ''Yuh know what's burning yer arses, boys? Well, I'll tell yuh. Yer jealous of Lebeuf like goddamn sons o' bitches. 'Cause it took him to get yuh guys a pay raise and get Bouboule back on the job. That's yer problem for Chrissake!''

The sweepers had split, disgruntled, and Lebeuf had been able to reach the back of the barn without being seen.

But after that incident, even Bill had shown reticence. They still went for an occasional drink together in the morning after work. But Bill never mentioned his job or his friends. Their conversation dwelt upon trivia, especially since the sweeper, with a rather embarrassed air, had broken the news that Gisèle was to attend the convent boarding school and that the parish priest had promised to ''give them a hand.''

Lebeuf had not seen the young girl during the whole summer. How could he get in touch with her? School was over, she was not working at Mr. Sillery's, and Jules did not want to write to her. Until September, he had hoped for a letter or even a call from her. But nothing. Her mother must have forbidden her to get in touch with him. Lebeuf had wandered in the Maisonneuve district with the vague hope of meeting Gisèle, but to no avail. Perhaps it was better this way. What would seeing her do for him? She was not wasting away in a factory, that was something. The courses she was now taking were doubtless ill-adapted to her talents, but what could one do? *Another talent wasted the same way so many others are* reflected Lebeuf. He thought of her at night while making his rounds, but like some teenage chimera that one may as well soon forget. *She was not the girl for me.*

Sillery had also disappeared. Jules had met him three or four times downtown after Weston's departure. His conversation had been slightly less outlandish than usual. Jules had begun to warm to him when Augustin had decided overnight, at the end of the school year, to leave on a trip. As he had declaimed to his student friends during his going-away pow-wow at the Venus — he was going to bury himself "like Rimbaud in the African deserts, in the shade of the flowered palm trees to dance the Congolese carmagnole, with congenial cannibals, to the tom-tom." Since then Jules had not heard from him. He was deprived even of that company.

After failing his philology course, Lebeuf had not gone back to university. Yet a month's work would have sufficed for him to make up that course. Then he would have had his degree... But what was the use? He did not want to teach in the *collèges* of Quebec.

Lebeuf shrugged the thoughts away and, taking a key that hung from the ring slung in his leather belt, he punched the clock. On the hour, except at three and four o'clock, he had to make his round, punching the meters at the four corners of the Hochelaga plant. At an average pace each round lasted about forty minutes. But if you ran you could get it over with in about twelve or thirteen minutes. Lebeuf often chose the latter way. One night, Stevens' assistant, who received each of the punched rolls, had paid an unexpected visit to the new foreman. He had been curious to see by what machination the punching from one clock to the next showed an exact interval of three minutes. He had left without making any comment. Thus, Lebeuf could keep forty-five minutes of every hour for himself. At first, his running through his round had put him a little out of breath, but now it was not so bad. Forty-five minutes an hour was theoretically a lot. Of course, it was not fair to count it as forty-five minutes. Jules also had to check the cars for cleanliness and keep an eye on the men. But he still had enough free time. He would often withdraw to the shack, while the sweepers were absent, to read or daydream. He read a lot. However, he was continually obsessed by the thought of the coming round and that spoiled his pleasure. He was forever glancing at his watch or foolishly keeping an eye on the door to see if one of the head-office bosses would show up. What a difference with how it had been before, when he could enjoy three or four hours of leisure over there in one of the American-made cars!

Lebeuf pulled out the key from the punch clock, yawned, then walked toward the next station. Today he did not feel like running. Besides, maybe time went by faster when he walked out like this in the blood-whipping, chilly wind. Moreover, too many ideas were running around in his head tonight.

This morning he had received a letter from Weston which he almost knew by heart now. The American did not write often. He had gotten himself a job on a St. Louis daily. He had to glue down little ads on large sheets of paper for the lay-out. That freed a typographer. And sometimes, as a special favor — when the "real" reporters were busy on something — he was sent to cover miscellaneous items: a brat who had smashed his face falling from a balcony or some debutante who was going to wear an original dress. The job gave him a net $32.76 a week. He had closed this letter inviting Lebeuf to come to his paradise of journalism, where the beer was weaker than in Montreal but, in compensation, whiskey was cheaper.

Lebeuf sadly shook his head. *Too bad Weston doesn't live here anymore*. Sometimes he felt like dropping everything and jumping on the first train for St. Louis, without forewarning Ken. What a surprise he would have! But all that was nothing but reverie. He would not leave Montreal. He would not drop Marguerite suddenly, just like that. Too often he had promised himself to do so. Now he knew what to expect. The affair would drag on and on and on until they grew fed up with each other... *Unless things end up in marriage...* Anything was possible.

Their relationship had improved. Jules did not go out as much and Margot kept her mouth shut whenever he wanted to "work." He merely had to say that it was "for the company." Now that he had become a foreman, the waitress thought highly of his capabilities. But that was not the only reason. In mid-August there had been a scare — Margot thought that she was pregnant. They had met the doctor together, as a true middle-class couple would. Margot had bought herself a wedding ring for the occation... Luckily enough it had only been a false alarm. But the worries shared and strengthened their ties. Now they were saving money, "for later on," as Margot would say. A hundred dollars or so per month. *Disgusting* thought Lebeuf angrily, as he clanged his keys... What was happening to all his literary dreams and to his vague wish to help his compatriots, to awaken the soul of Montreal? Although he had free time during the day, Jules had not touched his "novel." He was taking fewer notes than usual. *I must get down to it some day...* Often the big man missed his university days — days of carefree life with no responsibilities, long sessions spent in cafés drinking hard and talking hard. *Yet that was not real life either. I must go back to writing some day...*

Lebeuf stopped walking and ran his hand over his face. Now the sky was completely overcast. It was starting to rain lightly. His round was over. He had twenty minutes of free time ahead of him... *It's crazy to stand up in the rain doing nothing* he thought. He shrugged and trudged toward the shack, head hung low, his electric lantern swinging to and fro with the movement of his arm.